NAME OF
THE DOG

Also by Élmer Mendoza in English translation
Silver Bullets (2015)
The Acid Test (2016)

Élmer Mendoza

NAME OF
THE DOG

Translated from the Spanish by
Mark Fried

MACLEHOSE PRESS
QUERCUS · LONDON

First published in the Spanish language as *Nombre de perro*
by Tusquets Editores, Barcelona, in 2012
First published in Great Britain in 2018 by MacLehose Press
This paperback edition published in 2019 by

MacLehose Press
An imprint of Quercus Editions Ltd
Carmelite House
50 Victoria Embankment
London EC4Y 0DZ

An Hachette UK company

A CIP catalogue record for this book is available
from the British Library

ISBN (MMP) 978 0 85705 494 7
ISBN (Ebook) 978 1 78206 493 0

2 4 6 8 10 9 7 5 3 1

Designed and typeset in Minion by Libanus Press
Printed and bound in Great Britain by Clays Ltd, Elcograf S.p.A.

For Leonor

Man is too much.
JORGE LUIS BORGES, "Poem of Quantity"

. . . guessing is always more fun than knowing.
W.H. AUDEN, "Archaeology"

There is no immortality, only memory.
CARLOS CASTILLA DEL PINO, *Aflorismos*

Translator's Note

Name of the Dog is the third novel in a series set in Culiacán, a prosperous and sweltering Mexican city of nearly a million people, half an hour's drive from the Pacific and nine hundred kilometres south of the U.S. border. Culiacán, the Sinaloa state capital, lies far off the tourist track, surrounded by desert and irrigated fields. The city's elite still thrives on commercial agriculture, but the trafficking of marijuana, cocaine and heroin has long outdistanced the sale of cucumbers and chilli peppers. This story takes place at the end of 2007, when Mexico's president escalated his war on drug trafficking, causing rifts in government, a realignment among the narcos and a rising toll of bodies the police would prefer not to address.

CAST OF CHARACTERS

THE POLICE

Angelita, homicide department secretary

Briseño (Omar), commander of the Sinaloa State Ministerial Police

"Gori" (Gorilla Hortigosa), specialist in extracting confessions

"Lefty" (Edgar Mendieta), homicide detective

Montaño, homicide department forensic doctor

Ortega (Guillermo), head of the homicide department crime lab

Pineda (Moisés), narcotics department chief detective

Zelda (Griselda Toledo), assistant homicide detective

THE NARCOS

Arredondo (Carlos), head of an unaffiliated gang, patient of
   Dr Manzo

César (Valdés), nine-year-old son of cartel boss Samantha Valdés

"Chopper" (Tarriba), bodyguard and gunslinger for the Valdés family

The Chúntaros, unaffiliated gang, sworn enemies of Tenia
   Solium's gang

"Devil" (Benito Urquídez), former policeman, now bodyguard and
   hitman for the Valdés family

"Drysnot" (Cayetano Villa Solano), bodyguard and gunslinger for
   the Valdés family

Durazo (Nicanor), underling of the Pacific Cartel affiliate in
   Hermosillo

"The Hunk" (Antonio Gómez), underling of the Pacific Cartel affiliate
   in Tijuana

"The Hyena" (Wong), underling of the Pacific Cartel affiliate in Mexicali

Max (Garcés), chief of security for the Valdés family

Minerva, mother of Samantha, widow of former godfather Marcelo Valdés

Samantha (Valdés), also known as La Jefa, leader of the Pacific Cartel

"Tenia Solium" (Valente Aguilar), head of an unaffiliated gang

"Uncle Beto," member of Tenia Solium's gang

Valentillo, teenage son of Tenia Solium

OTHERS

Alvarado (Gen Atenor Alvarado), retired army intelligence officer and advisor to the President, Ugarte's superior

Dr Castro (Uriel Castro Arellano), dentist in Bachigualato

Col Félix (Domingo), father of Gustavo, colonel in the Mexican Army

Constantino Blake Hernández, lover and former fiancé of Lizzie Tamayo

"Curlygirl," waiter at El Quijote, friend of Lefty Mendieta

Enrique, brother of Lefty Mendieta, former guerrilla who lives in Oregon

Francelia, daughter of Héctor Ugarte and María Leyva

"Glasseater" (José Rodelo), bar entertainer

Gustavo (Félix), cousin of Jason Mendieta

Jason, eighteen-year-old son of Lefty Mendieta and Susana Luján

Lizzie (Tamayo), wife of Dr Manzo, lover of Constantino Blake Hernández

María (Leyva), wife of Héctor Ugarte

Mariana (Kelly), romantic girlfriend of Samantha Valdés

Dr Manzo (Humberto Manzo Solís), dentist in Culiacán

El Presidente, the President of Mexico

Quiroz (Daniel), star crime reporter for "Eyes on the Night" radio
    programme

Rodo, boyfriend of Zelda Toledo

The Secretary, a federal cabinet minister

Susana (Luján), one-time girlfriend of Lefty Mendieta, mother
    of Jason

Trudis, housekeeper and cook for Lefty Mendieta

"The Turk" (Samuel Estrada), former narco, boyhood friend of
    Héctor Ugarte

Ugarte (Héctor), ex-military officer, undercover intelligence agent

MEXICAN FOOD AND DRINK

Agua de jamaica: a sweet cold drink made from hibiscus flowers

Aguachile: Sinaloa-style ceviche made with fresh raw shrimp,
    cucumber, red onion, lime juice, ground chillies and water

Asado a la plaza: fried cubes of beef with cooked vegetables,
    garnished with lettuce and fresh cheese or sour cream

Asado sinaloense: another name for asado a la plaza

Ate de membrillo: quince fruit paste

Barbacoa: cubed beef and beef marrow stewed in beer with potatoes,
    onions, tomatoes, olives, chillies and spices

Bucanitas: Buchanan's Scotch whisky

Buñuelos: tortilla-shaped fried dough served with anise-flavoured
    syrup and powdered sugar

Cabrería a la ingelsa: bone-in beef tenderloin flavoured with Worcestershire sauce

Ceviche: raw fish in lime juice with chillies, onion, tomatoes and salt

Chakira: a non-alcoholic drink made from strawberry, kiwi and orange juice

Chiltepín chilli: a very small and very hot chilli pepper

Huevos à la Leonor: hard fried eggs with sour cream, dried ground chillies and sea salt

Machaca: marinated beef or pork rubbed with spices, then pounded, dried and shredded

Machaca de pescado: dried fish cooked with tomato, poblano chilli, onion, garlic and spices, then mashed

Michelada: beer with lime juice, powdered chillies and salt

Pescado zarandeado: fish marinated in chillies and spices, then grilled

Pibil: Yucatán-style meat or fish cooked in a banana leaf

Salsa mexicana: chunky hot sauce made of tomatoes, onions, jalapeño chillies and coriander

Tacos al vapor: tacos steamed in a double boiler

One

Room on the twenty-fourth floor of the Hilton Guadalajara. No
dogs no cats no. Those are your instructions, Señor Ugarte, and
I expect quick results. A lousy reproduction on the otherwise
blank wall, curtains drawn, lights dim. Permeating everything,
the tension of mistrust. Ugarte fixed his gaze on the three men
flanking the member of the presidential cabinet, Man Number
One, Man Number Two, Man Number Three: With all due respect,
Señor Secretary, that will be up to you; my job is to provide you
with information, what you do with it is not my responsibility.
The Secretary wore a black suit and had already tossed back seven
drinks. Sancho Panza belly. Ugarte wore a wine-coloured tie and
had not touched his beer. His sixtieth birthday had come and
gone, the party postponed: In December I'll make up for it.

A small office in the presidential palace a few days before. At
your service, Señor Presidente, sir, how is your señora? are the
children well? An assistant served them whisky and departed.
Listen up, Señor Secretary, I'm told your data is bullshit and of
course I can't rely on it, I want precision, exactitude, absolute dedi-
cation and results, is that clear? so I'm going to send you a skilled
operative, not one of our own, have him infiltrate that meeting; a
friend will help out, he wants to know who we're after and to offer
his opinion, we're not going to allow that, I even refused to let it
be one of his men; I need to know what happens at that meeting:

who's there, if the señora is vulnerable, to what point we can control them and what their plans are; I want to know their next moves. The President drained his glass and refilled it. Any of our agents could do that, sir, I have experts at this sort of thing; please sir, turn a deaf ear to my enemies, they evidently want to undermine me. You aren't listening, don't let them drag us into their racket, they need to know they've been fingered as the enemy, that the agreements are over, that they're confronting a state that is strong and powerful. My impression is that they understand that, sir. Well, you sure can't tell, I'm sick and tired of hearing that I want to legitimise myself, that the economy is collapsing, that we're a failed state, I need everyone to pull their weight and do their jobs; if you mess up, start thinking about some African country where I can send you as ambassador, I know you like giraffes.

That is what brought them to the suite at the Hilton, the Secretary nervous, his bodyguards alert. Ugarte, a former military officer linked to a powerful clique, did not work much for the government anymore, he had health problems and they took too long to pay: what's the story with bureaucrats, how can they be so bad at routine business? of course, when it's time to shoot off their mouths they're the first to start yapping. Yet he could not resist this chance to learn first hand what was up with the President's flagship initiative, the war on organised crime, and just maybe he would be able to fulfil the secret longing that crossed his mind half an hour before as he rode the elevator up to the suite; what's more, he never refused an assignment from General Alvarado, who had utter faith

in him and who sent him pibil and decorations made from hene-
quen at Christmas. Man Number One took out a cigarette. Black
easy chairs. Man Number Two grabbed it and crushed it with a
smile. What was going on? A war apparently launched as a public-
relations exercise was killing an average of 19.3 people every day.
What was the President aiming at? Well, that much was clear, but
what did the heads of the cartels want? Good question.

The Secretary, who had not dared take a sip when with the
President, now emptied his eighth glass in one gulp. We will put an
end to them, Ugarte, we've got this war won, the President doesn't
need to worry, the gringos are happy, their ambassador says so
without any prompting. So, why do you need to infiltrate a meeting of the notables? He knew he was taking a risk they might not
hire him. The Secretary glared at him for thirty-three seconds. My
boss wants to be sure and he's the one in charge, Alvarado recommended you, I don't know why, have you heard of the Mochis
Initiative? Should I have? By now Ugarte was fed up, he did not
want the official version of what the General had already told him
in all its gory detail and he was beginning to feel ill; he stood up,
held out a card with a cell-phone number to bring the session to an
end. I will only call once from this number, Señor Secretary, make
sure you answer. You think my telephones are tapped? Yours I don't
know, but mine certainly are, and this one I will use just the one
time. Don't worry, I'll answer. Man Number Three handed him a
card with the number for him to dial. Don't delegate it to one of
these well-dressed young men. The three scrutinised him, their
faces blank. Of course not, Ugarte, who do you think I am?

You'll want to know right away, it'll give you more time to use the information to your advantage. You think you're a big shit, don't you? Well, Señor Secretary, I am Catholic. And you go to Mass at the Guadalajara cathedral. He thinks I live here, Ugarte thought, and he stood up. Señor, I have to go. He handed the Secretary a second card with another number: So you can tell me the place, day and time of the meeting; I will only answer once. They contemplated each other. Fucking shit of a James Bond. Goddamned fourth-rate Fouché.

While two agents waited in the lobby to trail him, the former officer lay down in his room on the nineteenth floor. He was exhausted.

Alcohol is the only adviser that decides everything by flipping a coin.

Two

He hated going to bed without a drink because it made him sleep in. Hey, Lefty, don't make like you've got a private line to the Virgin, I need action now, remember, without me you're nobody. Enough, fucking body, don't mess with me. Why not? you think I don't have rights? You want to be kissed and cuddled and milked, right, asshole? Why would I tell you no when it's a fact; I want to see a set of legs splayed wide, whoopee, just the way you like it. Fucking degenerate. Come on, you like that. You're sick. A banging on the bedroom door and Trudis's voice jerked his eyes open. Lefty, get up, what are you doing in bed so late? up, up, you've got a visitor. He looked at the clock: It's really early. What do you mean early, it's nine o'clock, you're never here this late, did you get drunk? Oh, I wish. So get yourself together, no man should be lying down at this time of day. Faintly in the background he could hear "White Christmas". Trudis, what time do you think your beloved rockers get up? Don't make excuses and hurry up; we're in the living room. He put on his pants. What now? how many times have I warned those spongers never to look for me at home, a black T-shirt, I've told Zelda too, the David Toscana boots, also black. What a morning, I'd better pick up some whisky or I'll turn into a bear and hibernate till spring; besides, it's December, and in this city which knows nothing but summer it's time to think about another sort of season: the playoffs. Trudis was waiting at the far end of the hallway; she had

19

a funny expression, something festive was lighting up her face. For sure she thinks she's finally convinced me to get a Christmas tree, maybe she's already bought it and wants me to see it. Your Nescafé is ready, señor. Hmm, she's up to something.

Waiting for him in the living room was Jason Mendieta, deftly texting on his cell phone. He stood up when he saw him. Lefty knew immediately who he was and he froze. Worth shit. Mirror, mirror, on the wall. Our lives are rivers that lead to the sea, he thought, and he swallowed. What a character that Susana was, always struggling to be more than her body, even though that's why we all chased after her. Hi, I'm Jason. And I'm Edgar, what's up. Handshake. Both hands strong, nervous, moist. Same height, same features, same smile. Lefty with his hair a little long and unruly, Jason's spiky like an asterisk. Fucking Enrique, he was right on the money. How are you? Fine. They sat down. The kid had a papaya juice half drunk and Trudis set Lefty's Nescafé on the table in the middle of the room, next to a few pudgy Santa Clauses. Jason kept up his rapid-fire texting. So, how is your mom? She's thrilled, chatting nonstop with my grandma, they're catching up. How long since she last came? Four years, Grandma visited us three times, but she can't travel anymore. First time in Culiacán? We came here every year for vacation until my mom started a taco shop in Santa Monica and became a slave to it; she sent you this, he produced a smallish box tied with a Christmas bow. Uncle Enrique said you'd like it. It was the C.D.s of Bob Dylan's thirtieth-anniversary concert. Wow, what a great thought. Boys, would you like to eat breakfast now? Um, I hope you don't already have it. No, and please tell her thank you very much. Señora, I already had breakfast. The coffee is enough for me. None of that, Lefty, don't think just because this young man is here you're going to get away without eating the way you should, I'll make you a nice omelette with goat's cheese, chillies and onions, and for you another juice. This one is plenty, señora, thank you. Lefty was still in shock, the kid started texting again. Do sons really look so much like their fathers? yikes, they ought to look like the milkman.

When did you get in? Last night. By car? By plane. Ah, so any news of my brother? He's good, a bit fat compared to you. He must eat like a horse. He likes hamburgers with double fries and he puts bacon on everything, and he's always drinking beer, sometimes too much beer. Is he an alcoholic? Hmm, I don't think so, what I do know is how much he misses you, you can tell he loves you a lot; we saw him last Thursday and he got all nostalgic. Silence, except for "Jingle bells, jingle bells, jingle all the way". Enrique told me you were unbeatable in the mile. I do alright, but I'm not into that anymore and I don't train much. Don't you want to make the Olympics? Well, I'd rather be a policeman. Mendieta studied him, the kid was like him, undoubtedly an improved version, but that much? Are you sure that isn't like a kid wanting to be a fireman? No, I've thought it over and I've made up my mind. In the United States I suppose it's a good job, here it's usually a last resort. I don't know about that, I just know I want to be like you; several of my friends have decided to be the same as their fathers and I will too. Lefty's mouth hung open. Wow, this kid has it all figured out and he's not fooling around. Is that the latest thing, to be like your fathers?

Maybe, Jason read a text and responded immediately, maybe it's because some of them are real heroes, in Iraq, in Afghanistan or in the city. Trudis called them to the table.

Young man, tell me again what your name is, gringo names always slip away on me. Jason. Young Jason, don't pass up the opportunity to taste this machaca, it's special, nothing like the ones they make in a blender. My grandma already made me some. Well, now you can compare them, taste it, don't tell me you're like Lefty that way too, he eats like a bird; come on, just have a little, you need to grow up strong and healthy even if you are as tall as Lefty already, and she served him; he can eat his omelette and you can have this delight, taste these flour tortillas, they're made the way God wills, you need to feed that body. Trudis is not easy to contradict and as you can see she has great powers. Don't exaggerate. Jason took a bite and chewed slowly; Mendieta watched him out of the corner of his eye. So this kid is my son, well, alright, what can you do? that's some pedigree and on top of it all he wants to be a badge; I've got to call Ortega so he can tell me what's what, what a father talks about with his son, where he takes him, what advice he gives him; I'm not going to spoil him, no way could I take him to El Quijote; what an eager beaver, since I wouldn't return his calls he didn't let me know he was coming, he didn't want me to run away and hide, and that bit about him wanting to become a badge is heavy, isn't it? and Trudis is thrilled, they act like they've known each other for years, should I take him to the whorehouse? no, I don't think so, he must have his girl, he's not ugly and his face sure isn't pockmarked.

Jason was a strong boy, light-brown skin, sure of himself, he looked at his messages, answered rapidly or ignored them. I want a Christmas present, he said after finishing his juice. Lefty was still floating and Trudis was somewhere in the bedrooms doing her thing. I deserve one. Why? Because I'm the only one in my class this year who didn't do drugs. It's a big problem over there, isn't it? It's really hard to stop; if you want, you can do a drug test on me. They smiled. I brought you some American Nescafé, but you didn't notice the difference. Mendieta tasted his coffee. You're right, it's even worse. They smiled again and relaxed. Uncle Enrique warned me, he told me not to be offended when most of what you say is rude. Is that what that damned beer belly told you? wait till I get hold of him, tell him what he's going to die of. Listen, Mama wants to speak with you, don't think it's something I put her up to, all I wanted was to meet you and see what comes from that, and that's happened, I like you. His stomach started feeling weird. See me? for what? he thought, then suggested: How about the three of us have supper together tonight? Only I have something on for tonight, so you two go ahead, will you pick her up at my grandma's? Why not? at eight; if there's work to be done I'll ask someone to cover for me for a couple of hours. Will you lend me your Jetta? you probably go around in a cruiser. I'd rather give you the taxi fare, I don't want anything to happen to you, the city is pretty hot. They looked at each other, expressionless. Are the police that bad off? Bad off is putting it nicely, no-one can explain how we manage to function. Alright, just don't forget my present. Have you thought of something? Yup, I'll tell you later. Trudis went to answer the telephone, which was ringing off the hook. Hello; it's Zelda. Lefty put the portable to his ear, listened closely and said: Tell me the address again; O.K., I'll see you there in an hour.

Three

Ugarte was good-looking. Women chased after him and men liked to call him Faggot. In high school they said it so often that more than once he wondered: Could I be? Looking in the mirror he convinced himself he was more beautiful than his sisters, so he went to the Military College and soon stood out as a hard-ass. Then General Alvarado trained him in intelligence and he never made a mistake; well, one, maybe two: being honest and falling in love with the wrong person. The first obliged him to spend fifteen years in hiding until his enemies were dead and buried; the second brought him the best and worst days of his life and may have been what goaded him to make the most of his not inconsiderable talent. The army kicked him out, but the General fixed things so he could continue collaborating as a special agent, a privilege he was deeply grateful for.

Because loneliness kills more people than cancer, he always visited Turk Estrada, a narco doing twenty years in the Tijuana lock-up and a friend since junior high. Besides, it wasn't far from La Jolla, California. Estrada was short and fat, and during his time in La Mesa, despite the brutal physical and psychological torture, he never let a real name pass his lips; he invented so many nicknames and situations the jailers were convinced he was faithful as a dog. Later on he lived under protection in Culiacán, doing odd jobs, putting his children through school and dragging around a burden of hatred he could never shed.

What's doing, fucking Faggot? Ugarte heard his friend's greeting. They had arranged to meet at Vía Verde, a natural food restaurant, because neither of them wanted anything to do with alcohol, that three-faced con artist who pulls in so many parishioners. Christmas mood music. What's up, I.B.M.? That nickname twists my balls. What's wrong with it? you should be proud, Immense Bucket of Manure, how's the family? Great, next year my eldest gets his law degree and my daughter is doing journalism, what about yours? Same as last year, my daughter is still stubbornly insisting on an army career and her younger brother is a singer. Like Jim Morrison? you know his dad was in the navy. Not even if God wills, that guy was nuts, that's the last thing I'd want for my son. But he sang "Light My Fire" like he was God himself. My son's into other things, he wants to be in musicals and shows, nothing to do with rock. A waitress wearing a Santa hat served them chakiras, the juice that smooths and soothes, and turkey-and-cheese sandwiches. Did you celebrate your sixtieth? At home, with a barbecue in the back yard and agua de jamaica. Next they'll be doing a piñata for you. My son hired a violin trio, boring as hell; I told him: son, since you're messing with me anyway you might have brought something more danceable; nope, he says, because for his thesis he's drafting a noise-reduction law for the city, people won't be able to hold weekend parties at home or in the street, they'll have to hire a hall. If they approve that, good luck to the police who have to enforce it. It's going to be written in Chinese; and you, what about you? After Christmas or in January. Do it in January, there are too many parties in December and you won't enjoy it as much.

I'll think about that. Then they talked about the weather, about how women were getting more and more beautiful, how pale Ugarte looked and thinner than usual, and how bloody the war on organised crime was getting. Room adorned with Christmas decorations, "Let it snow, let it snow . . ."

I need to ask a favour, Ugarte murmured deadpan, taking a sip of his juice; he had not touched his sandwich. Estrada stiffened, his dark squint acquired a rather strange glow, somewhere between fear and ruthlessness, he stopped chewing. There's some money in it, not much, but within the realm of decency. You know which side I'm on, fucking Faggot, no shit is going to make me cross over. You're looking at me like I'm about to take a swing at you. I'll never get over that mother-fucking crap; before, what I wanted was to stop being afraid, I wanted to forget, now I couldn't give a shit, there's no fixing it. Do you still wake up at night? Sure, but I don't scream anymore, so I don't piss off my old lady. It's not about fingering anybody. It was your grandmother, asshole, straight up, I saw her with these very eyes the worms are going to eat. I haven't forgotten your tricks, I.B.M., you lie to delay. O.K., what's itching that head of yours? In a few days there'll be a meeting of the king-pins or their deputies, and I need to be there. So what the fuck does that have to do with me? You've got connections, I know. Who's connected is your fucking mother, I told you I cut all ties, it's a fact. Don't get scared, this is just a routine thing. You don't say, and then we'll go out dancing with our respective wives? All I'll find out is if anything important is agreed. In other words, it's a big fat fart of a deal. Maybe, though nothing compared to what you and I have lived through. You're going to take another stroll between the horse's hooves. Just to dust myself off. Are you going to name names? No way around it, but only to say who was present. The Turk, on edge, was thinking about a crucial meeting held the day before at dusk in the Hotel Paraíso; well, no flies escape from a closed mouth. The Turk made a mocking face: Don't tell me you agree with this stupid war that just piles up slabs of cold meat? No, not me, and I want to help put an end to it, am I wrong? besides, we're sixty, we should have some fun. The war means shit to me, I couldn't care less about it, they say it's a fight picked by the President, who according to my son has a screw loose. Do you think it's right so many young dudes are getting killed? Fuck them, they want to get into the sauce? well, let the assholes learn what it means to love God in Indian territory. They fell silent, in the background "When I'm Sixty-Four" with orchestra. They're talking to you, Faggot buddy. They're talking to us, I'd say. Just then, a family came in to have breakfast, the father and mother looking around apprehensively before sitting down. Whose deputy do you want to be? The one in charge, somebody I can charm. If only the kingpins show up, you're fucked. I know, that's where I want your help. Fucking Faggot, you like the wicked life. It's one way of feeling alive, isn't it? Fate is a fucker. And she gets up late. I'll ask around, and like every other time I've given you a hand, I don't know shit about it, and you should hang up your balls, Faggot, we're too ancient to be playing cowboys. It's to keep our joints from seizing up, you know what they say, any organ you don't use atrophies. But we aren't organs, don't bullshit me, the nearly twenty years I did was enough for me, and with the fifteen you did you don't owe anybody anything either. You're just like my wife. Ugh, if mine finds out she'll cut off my balls. They smiled. I can hardly believe you want to get mixed up with the Tricksters. Give me a hand and it'll be a breeze, you'll see; I'll come by here every day between five and six until I see you, I prefer that to the telephone; he handed him an envelope with money. Transparency makes for friendships that last, and it's your turn to pay, fucking Faggot. What, weren't we going Dutch? Dutch my balls, pay and let's get out of here, they've thrown us out of better dives. "Jingle Bells" by Boney M. on the sound system.

Four

People are their habits and, if you really want to know, that was what did Dr Manzo in; he was always last: last to leave, last to finish his exams, last to get married, but he was first to be worth shit; tell me this: what would he have lost by slipping out now and again to have a few beers with his buddies and letting his receptionist close up? Nothing. His assistant would leave first, then his blonde greeter and, a little while later, him; it never failed. That's why it didn't surprise me when I heard he got laid out on a platter, meeting the dawn in his dentist's chair like a lapdog, with a bullet in his head . . . He wasn't in the chair? same difference, he won't get over the dead part . . . I wonder about that, in school he was insufferable, but nowadays who could hate a guy like Manzo? he didn't mess with anybody, he'd changed so much you might say he'd become a nice guy, and with that babelicious wife? Somebody with very black blood, that's who. When business was good I'd stay late and see him leave, now that everything's upside down I leave whenever I feel like it, and it makes no difference. This country is a piece of shit, tell me it ain't so, deep into a war that's going no place fast, fifty million living in poverty and maybe sixty million unemployed; are you hiring at the police? . . . No kidding. It could have been a mugging, these days they'll do it for pocket change and he was a dentist who had patients every day; well, more like a torturer I'd say, yup, he dangled my fate in front of my eyes for a porcelain

30

amalgam, claimed the metal filling I had was leaching mercury, poison; but what dentist isn't? Seems like they enjoy that part, the bastards. If it wasn't robbery he must have screwed up with a patient, I'd bet there were several who had sworn to get him; but really, what bad news, I was supposed to go for a cleaning next week and he always charged me half price, you see we were in high school together. What can I get you? the storekeeper turned to a young student who had come in. A light bulb. How many watts? The special ones. A special light bulb, who do you think we are, asshole, if you think we sell garbage so people can get high, you're nuts, get out of here, you idiot. But. Get out! Mendieta smiled. So you sell light bulbs to the crackheads, that's interesting. Don't pay any attention, officer, that asshole was messing with us. Well, this is simple, like in the classics you get to choose: imprisonment, banishment or burial. That's fucking classic, let's get one thing clear: yesterday I left early with my buddies, I'm not the kind of guy who gives advice and doesn't follow it.

He felt at peace. Christmas brings work, presents, parties, good weather, relaxation. Families get together, friends call, patients are thankful. You can eat just about anything without regret. Jesus allows that and more. Diet? Well, I'll start on Monday. His thoughts ploughed ahead: after Christmas, Mazatlán, a stroll on the beach, grilled fish, swordfish ceviche with carrots, cold beer. His wife loved that. The patient, a good-looking woman of about sixty, spat out a gob of blood, rinsed, breathed in, the assistant filled the little plastic cup, and he went back to extracting a left molar. The last of the afternoon. He would buy a Juan José Rodríguez novel and something by Anton Chekhov, who was also in the health profession, and he would feel like somebody else. He loved feeling like somebody else, acting like somebody else, even when he was making love his wife would catch on and her moans and whispers would be nothing like the pitiful sounds she exhaled when she did it with him as himself. Hey, you ten-peso whore, I'm Johnny Depp, are you planning to ask about "Edward Scissorhands" or "Pirates of the Caribbean", or are you going to pull down those panties? Did that hurt, Señora Frida? we're almost done, you can rinse now, please. The blue mask muffled his voice.

Again, he thought of his wife. I hope you've got on the ones with little hearts, Brigitte, they make you look the best. I'm wearing the ones you gave me for my birthday, Alain honey, in other words, nothing.

Minutes later the patient, looking pale, left the office; the assistant departed next: See you tomorrow, doctor; and the receptionist three minutes later: I put everything in the safe, tomorrow first thing we do the wisdom teeth of the undersecretary of the economy, remember him? he sweats like crazy. Did he pay us in the end? He promised to settle the account on Friday; see you tomorrow, doctor. Goodnight.

He smiled, spent a few minutes doing nothing, then freed him-self of his tie; he was about to hang it up when he saw him in the doorway. Are you leaving now, doctor? It's been a long day, that's for sure. Before you go, pull this tooth for me, the fucker's killin' me. He was wearing jeans and a blue T-shirt that said "LONDON" across the chest. We're closed, señor, I'd be happy to do it tomorrow, we open at nine, if you can come at eight I'd be delighted to take you then. Don't even think about that, you do it now or you're going to be worth spilt cum; burly, dark-skinned, darker scowl and a chip on his shoulder. Sounds in the waiting room. He peeked out and saw four armed thugs resting absent-mindedly in the easy chairs and at the desk. Two were snorting coke, another was smoking and the youngest was writing on a big piece of cardboard. He noticed a bulge under the T-shirt of the pushy patient and he began to tremble. My assistant just left and I can't do it without her. Stop fuckin' around, doctor, any of these jerks here can be your assistant, ow, fuck, I can't stand this bitch. Is it swollen? Like I can feel a lump, it's been growin' and growin' for the past week. Open your mouth, he left his coat on the chair. He looked. Alcohol fumes over a strong stench of rot. You've got a huge abscess and it's really inflamed, but hang on until tomorrow so we can take an X-ray, and I'll have to operate, are you allergic to anaesthesia? What fuckin' tomorrow, doc, understand me, this prick has me fucked, take the bitch out now. Pounding heart. Señor, understand me, the way it is, it's impossible to extract, I'm going to give you some pills to reduce the inflammation and we'll do it tomorrow. Fuckin' mother, are you ever stubborn, he pulled out his gun. Does it ever piss me off when people try to pull pricky shit, and he shot him through the heart.

The echo snapped like an athlete's knee.

And then it was all remembering: a quiet life, his wedding in Santa Inés, make-up at the last minute, the coloured rice flying, fiesta at the Country, honeymoon in Hawaii-Five-O, how much he liked Chespirito and plum ices and that blue bicycle his father wouldn't buy him when he was in junior high, where everybody hated him because he was a top student and he wouldn't let anyone copy and because he was afraid of horses and his parents never let him go to sleep without saying his prayers.

Edgar Mendieta contemplated the cadaver of Dr Humberto Manzo Solís. Dried blood over the heart. Two bullets in the chest and eight in the abdomen. Ortega and his people working, the forensic doctor hurriedly writing his report. Christmas decorations all over. Lefty, I'm so glad you got here, I've got to go. Fucking Montaño, have you realised how skinny you are? Uh-uh, I'm perfect, besides, I've got news for you: I bought a house for socialising, no more wasting money on motels. At last you're going to get rich, you bastard. Whenever you want, it's yours. Are you using it already? Of course, I gave it to myself for Christmas and I'll be there in just a few minutes to break it in. What about this guy? he pointed to the body lying supine decubitus on the floor. Shot in the heart, the bullets came out his back and he's been dead between twelve and fourteen hours; the ones in his stomach are extras, none of them fatal. What would he have been doing before he died? the detective wondered, dentists don't smoke in their offices anymore, maybe he was sucking on a candy or he called his wife; from the look of things he didn't put up a fight; given the hour he must have been alone, of course, anybody here would have called us or we'd have two bodies to deal with. Friend, I'm leaving him in your hands. Did you know him? No, but people say he was a good dentist.

Congratulations on the house. "Jingle bells, jingle bells, jingle all the way," a technician sang as he worked. Ortega came over, in his palm he held two big lead slugs and eight smaller ones. Why would they have used a Herstal on him? he was a dentist, he didn't wear a bulletproof vest. What about the others? All .45s, shot into him when he was already dead, according to Montaño, there are dents in the floor, the big ones hit the wall. Maybe he didn't have another gun? An ingenious response, now I finally understand why you're the detective. Have you seen Zelda? She's in that office interrogating the receptionist, who was the one who called. No signs of struggle, his coat is on the chair, Jack the Ripper everywhere. Near them the singing technician was picking up a few grains of white powder, another was taking photographs, a third looked for fingerprints. Tell me something, Ortega. Hey, hey, no way, I'm just here by accident, Papa, not a day goes by when we don't have more bodies than we can deal with, so don't start in with your "Do me a favour since we're friends." What a fucking twerp you are today. I know you inside out. Just one question, and it's not about work. Listen, jerkoff, I don't like to stir shit up, you know that. What do you talk about with Memo? The crime-lab technician opened his mouth and thought for a moment. You're going to change jobs or what? More or less. Now that you ask, we don't talk much and when we do it's about soccer, he's nuts about Chicharito. That's all? Well, what else? no way I'm going to tell him about crime scenes or the way the bodies look, what's with these questions? Curiosity, do you lend him your car? Some nights yes, some nights no. What are you going to give him for Christmas? Listen, what kind of shit, are you going

35

out with somebody who has a son or what? Pardon me, señor, I didn't think this was top-secret stuff. A son is hell, asshole, he'll make you pay for all your sins, the sins of your past and the ones you'll commit a hundred years from now, but the only people who know are people who have them, and if you have three it's three hells, if not more. So, what luck I was born sterile. And if you lend him your car you've got to give him money for condoms, fucking kids aren't satisfied with just partying, they always want to dip in the brush and they couldn't give a shit about the bitch of pregnancy. Hey, hey, it was just a question, take it easy, I can see I touched a nerve. A nerve? it's the witches' Sabbath, you bastard, give thanks to God it didn't happen to you.

"They say distance brings forgetting," sincerely, Luis Miguel.

He went into the office where Zelda Toledo was finishing with Noemí Campa, the blonde receptionist, who was distraught and unable to formulate anything useful. In the other chair sat Lizzie Tamayo, the young widow, sobbing. Stay where we can get hold of you if anything comes up, Zelda said, and she told Campa she could leave. On the wall, a few prancing reindeer from Unicel.

Lizzie: Thirty-five years old, 35½-24½-36, high-school beauty queen, two semesters in business admin at the Tech, no children; she married Manzo to spite her lifelong boyfriend, she likes Madonna, Mecano and Maná, she adores sexy clothes and soap operas, her lover is named Daniel, Dani to her, though two or three times a week she also goes to bed with her old boyfriend. In high school she was in a play in which she whimpered the whole time: she was recalling that just then.

Mendieta watched her and felt a great weariness. Her expression said nothing, and he could guess her answers before Zelda asked: Did your husband tell you about anyone who hated him?

Mendieta (in his mind): No.

Lizzie: Yes.

Mendieta: Oh, shit, I was wrong; besides, she's a knockout, the vixen.

The detective was now paying attention; he waited a few seconds and she did not add a thing. Who are you speaking of, Señora Manzo? Zelda eyed her suspiciously. Who hated him so?

Lizzie: His father, when he was a boy he never bought him a racing bike and his Christmas presents were never what he wanted.

Mendieta: What to get Jason is a riddle; what has a face and two hands and it sits on the wall?

Zelda, at a sign from Lefty, continued the interrogation without missing a beat: The man's address?

Lizzie: He died two years ago, but he hated Humber, in fact he never treated me right, he didn't like my style, he liked to put me down.

She sobbed. The detectives carried on for a few minutes more, during which she filled them in about Dani and the lifelong boyfriend, including their home addresses, plus the fact the dentist had no mother, no siblings, just a couple of cousins in Puerto Vallarta they had seen only once.

Where are the journalists? especially Quiroz. Strange they haven't come, boss. They only care about mass murders, one body isn't news anymore. It's been a month since we last saw your friend,

I can't wait to hear you chew him out next time he shows his face. I hope they've kidnapped the fucking pest.

They left the place with a list of patients, suppliers, etc. At the door, Noemí was sending home the people who turned up for their appointments and once everyone was gone she locked up. The undersecretary of the economy went off so sweaty he was practically transparent.

Mendieta talked to the owner of the hardware store across the street, a former schoolmate, who provided some information on Dr Manzo's routine. He asked Zelda to interrogate the lovers while he dealt with the list. What sort of patients would be snorting coke in the waiting room? The technicians said it looked pure. Isn't that incredible about Jason, besides, I'm going to have supper with Susana Luján, let's see if she comes wearing her short skirt and no underwear. Oh, Mama, may God hear you, do you remember her mole right up there? Shut up, fucking body, you're the worst of the worst, you can't even look at a girl without wanting to get her into beddy-bye. Listen, this girl Lizzie is tempting, isn't she? Take it easy, you fucking leper, you wouldn't leave a single one to be the maiden aunt.

Before getting on the road to Headquarters, he ate an octopus and shrimp cocktail with lots of chiltepín chilli at Roberto's, the best spot for seafood. When the news is always the same it isn't news, that's how it seemed to him: twelve bodies found in various places around the state, the army patrolling, the police terrified, the politicians declaring that no-one needs to worry because they're only playing cowboys, and the country burning. It becomes normal, and what's normal doesn't encourage reflection. At his desk he put the newspaper aside and dialled Enrique: What's up, beer belly? Tell me the kid doesn't look exactly like you. I just met him and I like him a lot. Did he already tell you he wants to be a policeman? And that he's in a club of young guys who want to be like their fathers. Fucking Edgar, you sound excited. That's why I called you, so you can hear how I feel. He's a good boy, treat him well, he deserves it. Don't worry about that, besides, he has our genes all over him. He likes to be with the family, he's been great with my girls, he even gives them presents. Takes after his father, no doubt. Congratulations, bro, and don't be a fucking skinflint, give him money so he can have a good time. Will a gazillion be enough? Don't fuck with me, you should rise to the occasion. I shall be a Modelo father, don't you worry. A Tecate father would be dynamite too. O.K., see you later, I've got to catch a drug lord. Don't make me laugh. Lefty hung up, then he took out his notebook with the list, Lizzie's backside came to mind, her generous bosom. Who was it who said the neckline is what best dresses a woman? And he saw he only had contact information for the lovers. Noemí swore he was an exemplary man and his patients adored him. Ofelia Anchondo, the assistant who came in later, didn't offer any clues either. An impossible case? My balls, these days everything is predictable, same story the weather or a gunfight or a wedding. Ah, no shit, tomorrow Devil Urquídez is marrying Begonia, and I promised to go. Alright, let's see, Papa, who were you torturing in your chair? Anayansin I., Attorney De la Rocha, that jerk, isn't he under-secretary of the economy? no wonder we are the way we are;

Carlos Omar Pérez, María Paredes, Martha and César Fuentes, Samuel Estrada, Daniel Quiroz, look at that, and here I was thinking that ink-shitter never even bathes. He read on for three pages without seeing anything out of the ordinary. He called Angelita. Which of the boys is around? Well, Terminator just came in. Send him over.

My man Termi, read this list and tell me who you know or which one sounds familiar. The agent, twenty-eight years old, skinny as a rod, read slowly. I know Attorney De la Rocha, he's either really nervous or he's sick, because he's always sweating. Everybody knows that jerk, he's responsible for the mess the economy's in, but we can't toss him in the can, look at the others. Another read-through. Chief, do you know who Carlos Arredondo is? How would I know? They call him the Caporal and he seems to be more or less a heavyweight, we'll have to check. Those assholes have to go to the dentist too. They get sick. Right, let's see, according to this he has an appointment in three days, let's call him up. His number was on the list. On the seventh ring a female voice answered. Let me speak with Señor Arredondo. Who is calling? The office of Dr Humberto Manzo Solís. He's not in. Oh, he has an appointment for a cleaning. Who is speaking? Miguel Alonso, his new receptionist. Oh, it's just that a lady always calls. She's on Christmas vacation, excuse me, but did you study singing? Me? what kind of a question is that? It's just that you've got a powerful voice, it sounds like you've had training. I'm from the mountains and up there we talk loud. Well, you sound really good. Thank you. So, do you think Señor Arredondo will be in this afternoon?

Really, I couldn't say. Could you ask him? He's not here, he left two weeks ago, he called the day before yesterday and said he wouldn't be back until next month. Won't he spend Christmas here? He never does. Listen, are you sure you don't sing? Not even in the shower. The doctor wants to know if the man Don Carlos recommended is going to call. I don't know, I didn't know he'd recommended anyone. O.K., make sure you take good care of that voice, you could be singing in the Ángela Peralta Choir, merry Christmas. Same to you.

Zelda came in. Any news? Nothing, boss. My man Termi, find out who Arredondo's friends are, maybe one of them needed diamonds set into his smile. Don't forget the coat was on the chair, boss, he might have already finished for the day. It could be, but maybe this guy wasn't happy with how it turned out, he went back to complain and took him down, like his friend from the hardware store suggested; let's take a look at the patients from the last few days. The last one was Señora Valenzuela, Frida Valenzuela. Maybe it's somebody who just went there to kill him and was polite enough to wait until the last patient left. Good point, boss. What about Lizzie's lovers? Yes, I've got them in the little room. Let's see if they start fighting. They're friends, they're chatting as if nothing was wrong. Lock them up for a while and let's have lunch. Suppose the people from Human Rights show up? one of the guys is drooling about how well connected he is. You can make the case we police officers are poorly paid, poorly trained and poorly equipped. By the way, do you know when they'll give us our Christmas bonus? Agent Toledo, do I look like I work in Payroll? Sorry, it's just I need the money. Don't get anxious, it's bound to show up within two years.

They went to El Quijote.

Curlygirl wasn't there, he was on vacation until December 22. So they ordered beers, steak and potatoes, flour tortillas and salsa mexicana. I couldn't believe it, those guys turned out to be friends, Dani didn't know Lizzie still saw Constantino, and he just smiled, utterly unperturbed. That's what the democratic school system produces nowadays, Agent Toledo. Don't tell me if you had a girl-friend you'd be fine with her running around with somebody else. Well, when have we police officers ever been democratic? Maybe that's why I find it so strange, though the one getting gored was Dr Manzo. What did you make of the office, Zelda? With so much Christmas stuff I couldn't see a single clue. According to his school-mate, who by the way sells light bulbs for crack, the guy was alone; probably a patient turned up late and maybe didn't wait in the waiting room, which would mean he came with company; who would leave two grains of pure cocaine on the floor? A narco. Or his bodyguards. A blind man. An absent-minded professor. Some-body who had too much; besides, there's the weapon, he used a cop-killer. We're hot and then we're cold. So, what should I do with Lizzie's boyfriends? Most snorters are middle class or upper class; we should interrogate them, maybe one of them wanted to get him out of the way. Well, thinking about it, the girl's worth it.

At that moment the house band struck up "White Christmas" so the keyboard player could strut his stuff.

42

Five

Scottsdale, Arizona. Héctor Ugarte left the Scottsdale Healthcare Center on Drinkwater Boulevard, raising his hands in a gesture of resignation. Confirmed for the sixth time: his prostate cancer was terminal, they gave him two arduous months to live. That part did not worry him, way back at the College he had already made up his mind: in any endgame situation he would uphold military tradition and put a bullet in his head. Nevertheless, he wanted to render a final service to General Alvarado, the man who had taught him to appreciate his country, to understand the fragility of human life and to live amid corruption and narcos without getting tainted; besides, it was obvious he needed distraction. He thought about his contact, the Secretary, a man he did not trust.

Six hours later he landed at Pedro Infante Airport in Culiacán, Sinaloa, and thirty-four minutes later he was paying the cab-driver and walking into Vía Verde to sip chakiras with Turk Estrada. Fucking Faggot, you're never going to lose that habit of being on time, I got here seven minutes ago and today's only the second day I've come. There are vices that make you look good, I.B.M., being punctual is one of them. Those vices aren't for me, I prefer a well-rolled joint; sometimes I'm dying for a snort, I can feel the tickling in my nose and the urge just wells up inside me. So? So, I bite down on one of my balls, if I give in even once I'm fucked for good. You'd better buy yourself a plastic ball. Good idea, so I don't end up a boy soprano. The chakiras arrived, "Silent Night" on the sound system. Estrada handed him a piece of paper folded over. In case they're reading my lips, oh, and it's not the kind that burns itself up, eh, so let's have it back. Don't be so mistrustful, what can you lose? Fuck you, fucking Faggot; listen, buddy, you're like on the pale side, it'll do you good to get some sun. I'll need more than a tan to feel fit. Just don't go more faggoty. Or you more I.B.M.ish.

"Antonio the Hunk Gómez, Maz," he read, the Maz was extra and he liked that; he returned the piece of paper to his friend, who slipped it into the inside pocket of his jacket and waited before saying: He's a pretty boy who's always on the lookout for hot babes, he usually arrives early, he's from Tijuana and he likes the Sábalos Hotel. When is the meeting? Nobody knows. Thank you, you've earned yourself a double chakira, he put a grey envelope with the rest of the pay on the table. This is the last time we fuck around, don't forget it, if I want my relationship with the big guys to be on the up and up I shouldn't be asking questions that'll get me burned, you should have heard the groan from my buddy when I phoned him. What's the story, how did you find out? You know how it is, I made up a couple of things. I'm shocked, are you still mad at the Valdéses? Don't speak to me about those assholes, now with that dyke bitch in charge I hope they'll be worth shit; do you know who her gofer is? the son of Dwarf Garcés, remember him? the shrimpy asshole that got whacked the same night I got pinched. I remember. So I want nothing to do with those bastards; and don't play dumb, word's got around they did you one too. Don't make things up, they never touched me, I never felt affected. The two of them fell silent, the Turk trying to keep his anxiety in check. So, are you going to take a babe along? A pair, so they can play relay.

Ugarte entered his house in the Culiacán neighbourhood of Las Quintas. Leather furniture long out of style, pen-and-ink drawings on the walls, grimy knick-knacks on dusty sideboards, unkempt back yard overgrown with grass and weeds, not a Christmas decoration to be seen. He took his medicine and lay back in an old recliner that moulded to his body. For a few minutes he slept. Then he went into his study: bookshelves half empty, a cluttered work table, on the wall a diploma from the Military College and a few more drawings like the others; he opened his laptop, smiled as he read messages from his daughter Francelia and responded to them. The Turk was right, he had lost a lot of his allure, and to do this job he shouldn't be hard on the eyes. He wondered if he had bitten off too much, doesn't the General have someone else he can trust? Then he told himself to snap out of it; he wasn't just any old agent and the job was a special one; the more he thought about it the more he felt it was right for him. He skimmed the newspapers online: bodies piling up. The General's theories about the President wanting to consolidate power made no sense; for Ugarte it was nothing but a massacre, plain and simple, and the Mochis Initiative was a boondoggle to siphon millions up to the gods on Olympus. He wasn't fooled. In politics, as in life, only the strongest survive. And in a democracy that always means the wiliest, the ones best at disguising the gap between what they claim to be and what they really are. Success comes down to a single thing: you do whatever benefits the chief. Fifteen years he was obliged to spend in hiding because he thought differently and refused to bend to the power of the narcos and their mighty web of influence; if it weren't for Alvarado he might have simply disappeared, taking his not insignificant talents with him.

He recalled his dream from the previous night: I am in an ultramodern paradise, awash in electronic appliances and sweet-scented decorations. I'm happy, I like the place and I like what I see. I'm looking at a photograph of a snow-covered mountain on the wall when one of the machines spits out a hunting knife. It shines. It vibrates. I realise it's not coming at me and I breathe a sigh of relief, but only for an instant: it's headed directly at my daughter's heart. She's lying on a waterbed, I try to run and I can't, try to scream and nothing. María mocks me, and the red-handled knife continues flying straight at the girl, who's awaiting it with open arms, prepared to be sacrificed. No! I wake up bathed in sweat.

Remembering it made him shiver. He had no intention of telling Francelia, who lived in Cuernavaca with her mother and brother. Recounting dreams is for idiots, why should he? they're dreams, that's all, and usually irrelevant. He learned that at the college, where he had nightmares every night; the only time he tried to talk about one, his best friend told him to cut the nonsense. He returned to the recliner and gradually fell into a soothing reverie. He would do Alvarado's bidding, it would not be easy, not like before when he had all his wits and his name alone spelled trouble;

even so, he would do it calmly, drawing on the little strength he had left, before surrendering unconditionally to the inevitable.

Two days later he called the Secretary.

Six

Click. Whirrr. Constantino Blake Hernández, thirty-five years old, from Culiacán, degree in mechanical engineering, kick-boxer: I met Lizzie Tamayo in high school, she was my fiancée for three years until she married that jerk of a dentist. She left you to marry him? Something like that, I went to Mazatlán for the weekend and when I came back she wasn't my fiancée anymore. She must have had a good reason. You tell me: she wanted a doctor in the family, so she married a dentist. Is that why you killed him? Me? you aren't going to pin this on me; I hated the bastard, I won't deny it, but I got over it when we became partners. When you became his wife's lover. More or less. Where were you between eight last night and six this morning? Do I have to answer? You are a suspect in the murder of Dr Humberto Manzo Solís. I told you I had nothing to do with it, I agreed to come in because I wanted to see with my own eyes how fucked up you people are. So? So, I'd rather call my lawyer, I don't feel like answering such stupid questions. Use your cell phone. Long pause. No answer. You look like you've felt some intense emotions over the last few hours. Chuckles. Does it show? How long have you been Lizzie Tamayo's lover? For ever, I'm the only one who can satisfy her, when that bitch is with me she is the happiest woman in the world; she got married and all that, but as soon as she got back from her honeymoon our love life picked up where it left off. Were you with her last night when the dentist died? No, she wanted to have a regular time with him and why should I care? they liked to entertain themselves with silly stuff, they'd pretend they were other people. Do you know Daniel Peraza? We've never shared a beer or anything, but I think we get along pretty well. And you weren't with him the night of the crime either? Of course not; listen, I've had enough of this shit, if I can't get hold of my lawyer I want to pay the fine or whatever and get out of here, this place stinks. Well, go ahead and call him, I don't want them saying we twisted your arm to get you to confess. Silence. Something's wrong, this room, of course, it's out of range, you must think I'm an idiot, right? What did you mean when you said they liked to pretend they were other people? They'd play at being somebody else, for instance she'd be Marilyn Monroe and he'd be John F. Kennedy, and they'd talk trash as if they were them; Lizzie told me these things. Did she tell you about Daniel? Of course, I'm not the jealous type. So you have no alibi? Listen, don't shit on my balls, I didn't kill that jerk and I can't take any more of this fucking stench, maybe it's you that stinks, are you menstruating? Click.

After listening to the tape Zelda and Lefty sent Gori Hortigosa over to get the prisoner ready for a second session. Twelve minutes later one of the guards brought them the news: Gori was all keyed up when he went into the detainee's cell; buddy, he said, you should behave yourself, don't you disrespect my fellow officers; he was pacing around the cell and the guy just looked at him; here's something to make you behave like a person should, Gori said that, and then he threw a punch that caught the guy on the shoulder; you

49

shouldn't have done that, the buddy leaped up like a wild animal and boom-boom-boom, a punch here, a punch there and ka-boom, one in the face and down goes Gori, out cold, like he'd been hit by Julio César Chávez.

Lefty and Zelda followed him back to the cell. Two guards had carried Gori out and splashed water on his face, and he was coming around when Lefty walked up. My man Gori, are you alright? Lefty my friend, let me at him. Are you sure? how about you use your tools? No, I don't need them, Lefty my man, that guy knows how to punch and he did fuck me up, I concede that, now I want to use my right of reply, as they say. And suppose he wipes you out again? Then I'll resign, or you can put me to stapling papers or straightening up the files. What day is it today? The best of the year, Zelda my girl. Why don't we leave him alone for a while, until you're all recovered? Right this minute, Lefty, if you're going to cook it tonight, you've got to start soaking it now.

Seated on the concrete bed, Blake Hernández listened to their conversation with a grim smirk and a scowl. The cells on either side empty. Lefty hesitated. This bastard must have had military training, he looks really sure of himself and Gori is getting old. Gori, if you want to use the prod or something, he mumbled, you can go ahead. No fucking way, my man Lefty, I want a clean fight. Then Lefty addressed the prisoner: The señor wants a straight shot, any objection? None, let him in so I can fuck him up but good and you can let me go, I'm fed up with this pigpen. You're acting pretty confident. He shrugged his shoulders. Assholes like that are no problem for me, I meet two or three every day and I give each of them something to chew on. After hearing that, Gori stretched. He was calm, relaxed, and he asked them to open the cell door. It'll be like in the old days, Mendieta suggested, nobody hits anybody when he's down and whoever has had enough just raises his hand. Whatever, Blake said and he spat toward the door as his opponent stepped inside.

Detective Mendieta, a voice called from the doorway to the lock-up. It was Commander Omar Briseño, chief of the State Ministerial Police. The group froze. Lefty hurried over to him. Good afternoon, commander, what can I do for you? What kind of a circus is this? his eyes narrowed. We were discussing Christmas presents, did you see the little tree we put up? That guy I'm looking at, is that Blake Hernández, the engineer? One and the same, we were getting his advice, very interesting advice as a matter of fact, before we take him to the interrogation room; he's a suspect in the murder of Dr Humberto Manzo Solís, which we have been investigating since this morning. Does he have an alibi? If he does, he doesn't want to share it. I can see you asked for Hortigosa's help. It's just a formality. You don't say; you are going to do the following: take him to the interrogation room, have him tell you what he has to say without any funny business and then set him free; I got a call from his brother an hour ago, he's president of the National Commission on Human Rights and I don't want any problems, understood? It's crystal clear. Send me a report on the case, and I want to see you escort this guy out. Lefty returned to the group waiting expectantly. Agent Toledo, take Señor Blake to the interrogation room. Gori hung his head and let him pass. Standing tall, Blake left the cell wearing a cocky smile, the kind that gives you hives.

Señor Blake, we have taken note that you were born in silk diapers and that you have a lethal right hook; we've got no problem with letting you go, just tell us where you were last night. Lefty looked serene, he emanated a saintly aura of compassion. Are you an idiot or what? if I'd killed Manzo you wouldn't be able to lay a hand on me in your bitch of a life, but I had no reason to kill him, the guy supported Lizzie, he took good care of her, and he didn't bother us in the least; the real murderers here are you people and nobody chases after you, you fucking torturers. Get off your high balls, Señor Blake, we haven't treated you badly enough for you to be so prickly. I couldn't care less what you think, let me out of here before your dumbass nature rubs off on me. We don't want to have to invite you to stay for dinner, Señor Blake, tell us your alibi and there is the door. I won't say one syllable without my lawyer. We've seen how much he loves you, he won't even answer your call. I want out, I didn't kill that sucker and I've got no reason to be here. Mommy called, she complained to the boss. Don't you bring my mother into this, asshole, she lit no candle for this funeral, she's got nothing to do with it. From what I see, the one who lit a candle is her pretty boy. Let me out, this place gives me claustrophobia. Oh, poor baby, you know what? since I don't like whiners, you can go. Can I leave the city? Sure, but only with Mommy, you don't want to get lost. Blake gave him a fuck-you smile: I'll be at my company, Blake Auto Parts; if you need a trainer for your dog, I'll give you a deal. Lefty looked at him indifferently, but Zelda's expression was sour. We'll think about it.

The moment they left the interrogation room, the "Seventh Cavalry Charge" rang out from Edgar Mendieta's cell phone. Camel and Terminator were at Manzo's wake. All clear, boss, the Mass isn't until tomorrow at eight and from there to the public cemetery. Is the widow at her post? She hasn't moved, all very proper. Any suspicious visitors? Zero. If anything crops up, let us know.

Boss, I haven't seen you so cheerful in a long time, you look, I don't know, hopeful. It's the Christmas tree, seeing it makes me nostalgic and gives me happy thoughts. Zelda smiled, for a moment you also looked a little worried, something else that doesn't happen very often. It's your imagination, Agent Toledo, better you put your mind to calling Manzo's secretary and getting the contacts for the patients he saw yesterday. I already did that, boss, in fact I already interrogated them; Señora Eddy Quiñónez, who was first, says the doctor was a bit distracted, that she'd never bled so much. The assistant didn't mention that, talk to her again, maybe some detail got by us. Paty González said everything was normal, he was attentive, hard-working and very handsome. So nothing stands out. Maybe it was a narco or a hit man; there's the calibre of the shell and the grains of coke, and you'd have to be some kind of brute to take the life of a dentist who never bothered anybody. Montaño mentioned he had a good reputation, what did you make of Blake? Aha, I was afraid you would never ask.

Seven

The former military man checked into the Sábalos. At dusk he set himself up at the bar next to the pool, ordered a beer and did not take long to spot Hunk Gómez: a metre eighty tall, forty years old, slightly bulging gut, thick moustache, gold chain, gold bracelet encrusted with diamonds; he was wearing sky-blue pants, a white shirt, blue boots; and he was accompanied by three young beauties, one with long hair, another with it cut mid-length and the third cropped short. A fat bodyguard in dark glasses was keeping half an eye on him, while paying more attention to a couple of speedboats doing pirouettes a hundred metres off the beach. They were seated at a table with a variety of cocktail glasses and snacks, plus a half-empty bottle of Buchanan's. Mirth and merriment. Ugarte understood the man's character at a glance: demanding and vain, but willing to relax and have a good time. So he called a modelling agency and asked for a girl with no hair. They had none and sent him a short-haired girl named Katy Blue; twenty minutes after arriving, she was shorn to a stubble. The girl was sharp and $2,000 in cash dispelled any doubts on the spot: she was to walk slowly over to where the Hunk could see her, and that she did; she was to have fun with him, and indeed she did; she was to accompany him to his room for a drink with the other girls, and again she did her part; she was to take off her clothes, and at that point she nearly broke her deal with Ugarte. However, before the man took his third snort of coke, she had given him enough sleeping powder to keep him at peace until Sunday noon, since Ugarte had already called the Secretary and learned that the meeting would take place on Saturday at six in the Hotel Estrella Reluciente.

Would you like me to stay? The job completed, Katy Blue had found him sitting in the same spot, bathed in sweat. That won't be necessary, but be on hand in case there's something for you when my friend wakes up and wants to celebrate his birthday all over again. I'd love to come back, but only if it's for you, thin men turn me on. Got you, but you'll have to bring three friends for him, you can see he likes trios. As many as you want, do you feel alright? you're sweating, but your skin looks way too dry. It must be the magic of Mazatlán. Katy drank from his bottle of beer: This is warm, you haven't even tasted it, don't you like beer? They don't have the one I like. O.K., I'll expect your call. She truly was lovely.

Ugarte did not have the heart to recall how long it had been since his last real erection.

At that moment one of his cell phones rang. He saw the Secretary's number and did not answer.

Eight

Tenia Solium unceremoniously tossed a limp man from his double-cab pickup into the ploughed field and shot him with his pistol. He was already dead but had yet to serve his sentence. Fucking dentists, they're worth their weight in shit, they only want to take care of you when their fucking balls swell, with me those mothers are fucked. The young gunslingers on either side of him nodded. His son, a chubby sixteen-year-old who liked to leave messages on pieces of cardboard, spoke up: He deserved it, 'apa, I'm glad you didn't feel sorry for him, would you let me put a bullet in him? As many as you like, son, so you can get some target practice; shoot at his head or his chest, not his belly like the last guy. The youth shot the body of the dentist several times. Learn some respect, asshole, respect my 'apa. The others did not let their contempt show. The older man they called Uncle Beto put a hand on his shoulder: That's enough, Valentillo, save a few shots for later, we might have a big party. The kid smiled. They left the body in the cornfield with a sign on it – *sho some respet snaiks* – and found Tenia back at the truck spitting out thick wads of pus. What rotten luck, not a single bastard who'll pull this bitch. Boss, another gunslinger approached, the Chúntaros are in Bacurimí eating barbacoa. How many? Seven in view. Great, let's go get 'em. Should I put a sign on their bodies too, 'apa? Not them, my son, it doesn't do any good anyway. But I've got four all made. Ah, go ahead if you want, put 'em on any of 'em; Uncle Beto, I know you couldn't get it out yesterday, but if you don't yank this bitch for me I'm going to plant a bullet in your belly. Don't do that, boss, better let's see if there's a dentist in Bacurimí, we can kidnap him and we won't let him go until he does your tooth. Why would we let him go? better we kill him. You got it.

When they pulled up at the restaurant, their rivals were coming out with no long guns in view. At 'em, Tenia ordered, opening fire. Rrrat-a-tat. Oh, shit. Take cover. Run. Hit the dirt. Fuck it. Your father's here, fuckin' Chúntaros. The gang under attack responded with pistol fire; two of them fell dead, but the rest grabbed their Kalashnikovs from their pickups and pulled the triggers. Shouts: Follow me. Watch it. Over there. Three of Tenia's men rolled on the asphalt. People scattered. Diners in the restaurant sought refuge in the kitchen and got on their knees, praying; in the shops nearby everyone hit the floor. Neighbours crawled under their beds. About five hundred metres away a pair of policemen in a patrol car listened to the rat-a-tat-tat without apparent concern and continued calmly smoking. Is it behind us or in front, partner? Who knows? Bastards, what a waste of bullets.

Using the double-cab as a parapet, Tenia, a white handkerchief tied around his swollen cheek, and his son fired their A.K.s. The kid was reckless and his father liked that. No playin' sports or any of that bullshit, son, to be a real bastard with balls you've got to know how to pray and how to kill, in good times, bad times and the worst of times, just like your father. Yes, 'apa. Shattered windows, perforated doors and hoods, gas tanks dripping, bodies on the road, silence. The don of the Chúntaros, a man in a black hat, was seething: You're going to pay in blood, you sonofabitch. Of Tenia's vehicles one was ruined, so they piled their two dead and three wounded into a pickup that had a few inconsequential bullet-holes in one door and pulled out, merging into the uninterrupted traffic. The Chúntaros did the same.

Bit by bit, terrified neighbours peered out, called the police, who were busy keeping watch on another country altogether, and got ready to say they had seen nothing.

Some afternoons you just wish the earth was flat, tell me it isn't true.

Nine

From somewhere nearby a Richie Valens line wafted out: "You're mine, and we belong together". Lefty knocked at the gate of Susana Luján's house. A child asked what he wanted. Hi, I'm looking for Susana, Jason's mom. He was nervous, he felt himself sweating and clenching his rough hands. He had gone home first: a good scrubbing, clean clothes, black again, polish for his nasty, beat-up Toscana boots, plus a little Dolce & Gabbana Light Blue, and he was presentable. Come on, Lefty, you aren't even forty-four, asshole, you're quite the guy and you look good; you aren't ugly or handsome, in fact you're precisely the opposite. When Jason had shown up at Headquarters to borrow the Jetta, he'd advised him not to shave: You'll look cool and very sure of yourself. Zelda and Angelita raised their eyebrows when they saw the boy arrive, and when he left: Is he ever the spitting image of you, boss, wow, what a secret you were holding back, eh? Faced with two options, Mendieta chose the first: smile like an idiot; the other would have been to send them packing. Then he called Robles: Bring over the grey patrol car, the one without any markings or lights. Solián from Narcotics requested it for tailing someone. Shall I tell you what to say or do you know? Boss, I know, I'll have it here in a minute. Make sure it's clean as a whistle, I don't want to find some hairy scalp in the glove compartment. Are you going out with . . .? Hey, hey, take it easy, don't stick your noses where they don't belong;

Agent Toledo, I want you to analyse the statements by Constantino Blake Hernández, Lizzie Tamayo's lover-fiancé. Just like you told me; Daniel Peraza, the lover only, has a solid alibi, last night he was in Mexico City, today he came in on the eight a.m. flight; he's still got the boarding passes and the hotel bill. Unlike Blake, who didn't want to say boo. Manzo's patients seem like normal people. Uh-uh, Zelda, when there's so much violence, like now, there are no normal people, it brings out the worst in each of us. Your son is really handsome, boss, it's astonishing how much he looks like you. He's not my son, we're twins, it's just that he's an astronaut and he's back from a twenty-five-year mission in space. They smiled. Have you got a grandmother, boss? No, Angelita, why? Because she would be the only one who might believe that story. They smiled again.

My aunt says come in if you want, the child said from the doorway. Two minutes had passed. I'll wait here. The detective: What, is she hoping I'll have a heart attack? He leaned against the car and pulled out a cigarette. Is taking her sweet time a strategy? Match, puff, aroma. Did the people who outlawed smoking in public consider this situation? They must be incredibly confident, he blew out a cloud of smoke, or how would they get through this? They probably live by themselves, or they married young, or they only think about cancer and could care less about moments when you don't know if it's the death of Superman that's hit you or the end of the Lone Ranger. I'm happy, his body said, at last the touch of a miraculous hand to save me from this cruel void. Don't bug me, now is not the time for thinking about such things.

I haven't told you, but I still remember the night when the curve of her ass taught me the meaning of the word "sexy". Shut your trap, fucking skin-and-bones, you're worthless. You're the pest, you idiot. A black pickup with tinted windows turned the corner. Alert, but not turning his head, the detective observed its slow approach. Fucking narcos, what has anybody done to them to make them act out like they do? How does it help their business? If they want to settle accounts among themselves, who cares, but why drag the rest of us into their shitstorm? He pulled hard on the cigarette so they would see he was not afraid. Oh yeah, aren't you the hero. The vehicle drove by, accelerating a bit after passing Lefty, who recalled a scene from "The Warriors" when a gang member cruising slowly in his car and spoiling for a fight won't stop clinking the two bottles hanging from the thumb and finger of one hand.

As soon as he saw Susana in the doorway he crushed the butt of his second cigarette under his heel. S.M.P. Detective Edgar Mendieta, respected by colleagues, friends and enemies, teetered in the desert of his memory, mouth dry, mind dulled, the looking-glass through Alice. The first time I saw her she had four moles, he mused, one for each of the world's great capitals. My penis is going nuts, his body whispered, but Mendieta did not hear it. What can I say?

Susana Luján, forty-four years old, 35-24-36, an eighteen-year-old son, "looked more womanly and more girlish at the same time", as Almudena Grandes would have put it; and a tipsy Quevedo would have toasted her and muttered, "like a sword indeed, I reckon you'd / slay less sheathed, than in the nude", leaving his café

61

companions mute; and, well, her Chanel No. 5 arrived before she did with her frank and confident smile and a black skirt above the knee. Edgar, what a pleasure to see you, you haven't changed a bit. Lefty hurried to open the gate that had no latch. Hi, how are you? offering his hand, but she hugged him tight to show her pleasure was real and pressed her breasts against him so he would learn to drink tequila with lime and a bit of moonshine. She could not have been more than five foot two and she nestled for a moment into the chest of the man gingerly returning her embrace. God, help me until we get to where there are more people, help me to be me and not make a wrong move. Don't exaggerate, fucking Lefty, give her a squeeze so she can feel your manhood; come on, penis, be useful, make yourself felt. Dearest Malverde, Virgin of Guadalupe, St Judas Thaddeus, don't abandon me. Man, ain't this great, his body continued, barely audible, I'm getting hard so stop the bullshit, Mendieta, I'm flying high.

"You win nothing by trying / to forget me." Sincerely, Roberto Carlos.

You really do look good, Edgar, Jason told me you've got someone who takes care of you. Did he tell you Trudis insisted we eat breakfast? Yes, he liked her a lot, she made him feel at home. That woman is unique, he opened the door of the Toyota, Susana got in and there were her pale thighs, auspicious, insolent, between a promise and a threat … What year was it, that night when she was driving, Madonna's "Material Girl" on the stereo? We talked happily about everything, she was expecting a lot from life, she was eager to live, to be different. I was beginning to lose sight of my own fate, unable to fathom how a city and a decade can swallow you up, while everybody else goes on as if nothing happened. We're all ghosts haunting some street and it's harder to get in for history than for mathematics, she said that time in a honeyed tone; one day I want to be a chef, another a model and the next a stewardess, what about you? Carpenter, so I can have God for a son. But He's the son of the Holy Spirit, isn't he? You think so? Of course, look how I'm driving, she lifted her hands off the wheel and the car stayed steady in the lane. Hey, we're going to crash. We were going down Pedro Infante Boulevard at eighty kilometres an hour. No chance, look at my legs. Her thighs, she was steadying the wheel with her thighs, the miniskirt hiked up. Shit, why was she like that? Was such an assault necessary? Such an attack on reason . . . ?

What do you want to eat? Anything except tacos, could be asado a la plaza in the little market or grilled fish; you must have a favourite place, take me there. I have two: the Miró, where I can have breakfast, drink coffee and if Bety the owner is in she treats me as if I were the governor; and El Quijote, where there are roast-beef sandwiches and enough beer to get all of Culiacán sloshed. Someplace quieter. They went to Cayenna, a fusion spot the detective had never been to before. Nearly full. Little red candles on the tables. Christmas lights. They sat down where they could watch the river. Lefty, attentive, recalled her taste:

Waiter: Something to drink?

Mendieta (in his mind): A michelada with lots of ice and a steak.

Susana: A michelada with lots of ice and a tequila.

63

The detective smiled, asked for a Glenlivet, neat.

Appetisers? Duck tacos (in spite of herself) and shrimp in poblano chilli sauce.

This place is nice; listen, is the city ever spruced up, despite what they say about the violence it looks full of life. Well, today there are more funeral homes, and decent families buy more detergent. Don't be sarcastic, you know what? that's not how I remember you, you were a kid who read books and didn't get involved in politics. Susana had her own recollections: . . . What books do you like, Edgar? Anything except love stories. What do you mean you don't read love stories, why not? Who knows, maybe I'm just not interested. Aww, but they're beautiful. You read them? No, I don't read anything, I say they're beautiful because love is beautiful, isn't it? So beautiful there's always somebody committing suicide over it. Aww, but not very many, what are you reading now? *Conversation in the Cathedral* by Mario Vargas Llosa. A religious book, I can hardly believe it, you must think love is sinful. It's not about religion, it's a novel. Is it good? Well, I don't know, I mean I haven't managed to get into it yet. Why did you pick it? Because I read whatever falls into my hands, my friends and I read anything as long as it's not about love. I'll never understand that . . .

O.K., Edgar, to your health, here's to this moment after so many years. To your health, to the pleasure of seeing you; Lefty slugged his whisky and the waiter immediately refilled his glass. He sensed something strange and did not want to make a wrong move. Hey, behave yourself, Papa, easy does it, don't rush things. He looked at Susana: lovely almond-shaped eyes, fine features, her smile, her flirting, her small breasts. Fuck easy does it, Lefty, get your hands on her like I told you: let her feel your manhood. She looked happy, relaxed, but Jason had needs and she wanted to speak about that.

They ordered: Susana a T-bone with Worcestershire sauce and he seared tuna.

Adele's "One and Only" on the sound system.

When he was twelve he asked me for the first time who his father was. I'll tell you later. Even though he asked me often, he never made a big deal of it; anyhow in the end I told him his father was dead, and that was that until we ran into Enrique, who couldn't stop staring . . . Susana, did my brother and you really? Well, yes, what do you want me to say, it was an accident, and when I found out I was already living here and there was no other way to deal with it; you wouldn't know, but my period has always been irregular, sometimes I go months without one. Does Edgar know about it? Neither Edgar nor Jason. Don't you think you ought to set things straight? Don't jerk me around, Enrique, it's been centuries since I last saw Edgar, imagine if I were to turn up with this news. Well, you've got to do it, they're identical, that bastard was born all over again. Would you help me? For my nephew, anything at all. Can I tell you something, Enrique? he was born an American citizen and his last name is Mendieta Luján. That's outrageous, Susana, how did you manage that? A cousin took care of it . . . As soon as Jason knew he wanted to meet you, speak with you, ask you things; it really upset him when you wouldn't take his calls, fortunately Trudis told him all about your life; she's from the neighbourhood, isn't she? She's always lived on Bravo, about twenty minutes from my house.

Susana looked great in the dim light of the restaurant, soft music, her expressive eyes, the timbre of her voice, her Greek lips. Now, my man Lefty, don't let her wriggle off the hook. Talking so much about Jason made her seem more grown up and Mendieta took note, listened attentively and stopped thinking; only once did Dr Manzo, who did not deserve to die, cross his mind, along with his beautiful widow: could a narco have killed him? there were the specks of cocaine and the calibre was the kind they use. And now he's come up with this bit about wanting to be a policeman, what do you think? It's idiotic, I thought he was champion in the mile. He is, but he doesn't want to do that, you should see how they beg him to train and he acts like he has a private line to the Virgin; before we came he told his coach he wasn't going to race anymore because he was planning to go to the police academy and take up the same profession as his father. Your father? the coach freaked out, Jason, who's your father? The number-one cop in Mexico today, Edgar Lefty Mendieta. The man's jaw was hanging open. The detective could not hold back a satisfied smile, then he chewed slowly, revelling once again in his companion's enthusiasm.

I never thought I would tell you all this the first time I saw you, oh, and he also likes to read, and here's one big difference from you: he likes love stories. Really? Not long ago he read *Love in the Time of Cholera* and we went to the movie; he didn't like it, but I thought it was terrific, and his hair is like yours, as soon as it grows out a bit it gets all spiky. They had Rivero González wine with the meal and continued drinking afterward, she sambuca, he whisky, that fruit of Scottish witchcraft that helps him sleep just long enough. Do you remember when it happened? He didn't remember, I'd rather you tell me what I can do to help. I thought you were going to want a D.N.A. test. Maybe later, because I'll bet you dolled him up with mascara before he came to visit me. Susana put her hand on his. Both were warm. I want him to go to college; if he'd agree to race it'd be free, but since he doesn't want to we'll have to pay and it isn't cheap; we might manage to get a half-scholarship. Lefty was going to ask, How much are we talking about? but he let her go on. What did happen is that their hands cooled off and Susana pulled hers back; his body, which had experienced a tenacious pressure from the king of the crotch, returned, not without protest, to normal. If you help me convince him to stick with track, maybe you won't have to put up your part and we could have an Olympian in the family. What about him wanting to be a badge? Well, we've got to convince him to pursue the other option. What other option? Business, I'd like to see him running a big company, in the United States kids who major in that get rich in no time. So, does he want that? Well, I'd rather he explain it to you. For sure he doesn't, he thought, the fucking curse of the Mendietas, always working at something we don't believe in and resigned to living in poverty; maybe Enrique had options, but he didn't take advantage of them, now he's gone to fat and stuffs himself with beer and bacon, fucking pig; why didn't I finish my degree? right now I could be someplace else and still be worth shit.

They served them one for the road. Lefty knew she was done

67

talking about Jason, so now what? Would he take her home or ...? Better the or. But what should he do so the or would happen? Really what he wanted was to lift up her skirt, pull down her underwear, and whoopee, how do you like that? His body was screaming: Please, Lefty, don't let her go, you can see the babe is hot to trot. Don't hassle me, I've barely met her again and you already want me cornering her; it's true it's been a long time since you've been caressed, but take it easy, you've got to be patient; she used to be a volcano and she never held back, but as you can see, the years don't go by in vain, so calm down and act civilised. Don't give me that shit, fucking Lefty, pedal to the metal, grab her by the tits and see how she reacts. You're fucked up.

She took the initiative: Let's go for a drive, I haven't seen Culiacán at night in years.

In the Toyota, Lefty put on Air Supply, "All Out of Love", a teenybopper song he figured she would like and he hit the mark. Oh, Edgar, what great music. Lefty took her hand, which was now burning. They were still in the underground parking spot when Susana threw herself at him, kissing him wildly. That's the way she was, recalled the detective, who put his hands right in those flames that did not burn, but did they ever set him on fire. He turned off the Toyota. It was an armoured car with tinted windows, equipped for close vigilance and whatever else might come along.

"How wonderful life is while you're in the world." Sincerely, us. (Sorry, Elton.)

Ten

From his suite in the Estrella Reluciente, a four-storey, mid-twentieth-century hotel, Ugarte watched the sun descend over the wide golf course and the sea, and he winced at the thought of his coming demise. He moaned, it was too soon to leave this world, but nothing could be done, why celebrate his sixtieth? Estrada could do it, but not him; after two years of constant pain he was at the end of his tether. He made no effort to keep his eyes from welling up and the tears flowed. Ah, life, so often I risked it and now I resist the end. The setting was beautiful, gardens filled with shrubs, palm trees and rose bushes. He noticed a few tourists heading out for a stroll or inspecting the golf course, and he asked himself: Why do I fear something so natural? Is there really so much more I have left to do? Maybe I was always a coward, a reckless man with no self-awareness, a henchman with no scruples, a dog. A man in a dark suit walked across the garden, reminding him of the Secretary's bodyguards. He saw children running about, young men happily drinking and girls in wet T-shirts; older women were now emerging from the shade where they had sought refuge to protect their skin; he recognised Samantha Valdés, the powerful boss of the Pacific Cartel, and her partner Mariana Kelly walking toward the beach, they really are inseparable. What about María, would she be in Cuernavaca? And he caught sight of Max Garcés and his crew of bodyguards, discreetly covering the terrain. His father was a nice guy, brave and reserved, but he loved his coca paste or whatever it was he smoked, and he did not always work as hard as he should have. Samantha's father, on the other hand, was a monster, although, he mused, maybe there was no other way to build such an empire; he admired how good she looked in a red beach dress contrasting with the pure white worn by Mariana, who to him looked fragile, angelic, almost winged. She will attend the meeting, General Alvarado had said gravely, her father never would have, he worked through his deputies, but she is something else, she likes to get her hands dirty, and the way things are, she needs to get across that she's the one in charge; the Tricksters also have to evolve, Ugarte. That much? We don't know where they're headed, that's why the President needs fresh, solid information, we know they invited every group from across the country, however, apparently none of the others will attend, only the ones in the Pacific Cartel, but they're no small beer, there'll be at least fifteen for sure. Alvarado paused and added: What might have seemed like a media ploy has turned into a thorny mess; as policy, war is a slippery slope, nobody knows which way to turn, least of all Samantha, who may not even realise how powerful she's become. Anything new about the Secretary? asked Ugarte, recalling his phone conversation. We believe he's after something, but it's all very murky, we don't know yet what it's about, the President was forced to name him and he doesn't know what to do with him, stay alert, you might uncover a clue. What do the Americans say? They must be celebrating, especially since it's our people who are doing the dying. Then he went over plans A, B and C, above all C, which was the escape option in case of emergency. 5.45 p.m. He saw the women were still walking toward the beach and the meeting was at 6.00. She won't go, he concluded, so who will take her place? He finished putting on his disguise: moustache, make-up, wig, white shirt with cufflinks and a black leather jacket; he didn't have to look like the Hunk. Carefully, he picked up his small Smith & Wesson Classic, saw that it had all five bullets and stowed it in the right-hand pocket of his jacket. He put himself in God's hands and walked out, a certain martial severity in his step. On the landing a Christmas tree blanketed in lights and red and silver ribbons welcomed him. He took the elevator down. At the door to the meeting room stood two guards with no weapons in view.

Has the señora arrived? She postponed the meeting until eight o'clock. Oh, thank you, is everything alright? Yes, señor. Good, we'll see you a little later, and he headed back to his room on the third floor next to the elevator. The men continued their quiet conversation.

At the beach, Samantha and Mariana took off their shoes so they could walk freely. The sun in its final splendour and the cool breeze lifted their spirits. Several tourists were doing the same. A few young gringos were smoking marijuana and reading Allen Ginsberg out loud ("I saw the best minds of my generation destroyed by madness, starving hysterical naked . . .") sprawled on the sand holding glasses of tequila with Coke. Hour 33, when everything is a mirror. Are you going to the meeting? You know, I feel like sending Max; those guys, when they don't wear me out they get on my nerves, besides, they only sent their deputies and I need to speak with my son. I think you ought to attend the meetings until they all understand you're the boss and they can't push you around; you can talk to César before you go. You are a good adviser, Mariana, who would have thought. I know you like power, it makes you feel special, even unique, and happier; well, I want you to have that and enjoy it; the time will come, like it did for your father, when you can send a deputy. Suppose I send you? Oh no, I'll just stand at your side; before I forget, Devil Urquídez is getting married today, and his present is on its way, just how you wanted it: the keys to a house in La Primavera; he'll get them when they leave La Lomita where the wedding is taking place in . . . half an hour more or less. He's a good boy, that Devil. And very Catholic.

A few metres behind them, Max Garcés kept a close watch, the women's shoes in one hand. Without relaxing his surveillance of the entire terrain, he was revelling in the fine weather. He had been born in the mountains and the sea was always a discovery. His men moved strategically, a few walking in the shallow water, others on the beach and seven on the golf course. Protecting Samantha Valdés was his life, and all his men were prepared to give their lives for her.

At sixteen minutes to seven, before darkness set in, they turned back. Samantha and Mariana walked in sync, their arms around each other. They were planning out their lives, the year to come, a vacation. La Jefa was aloof, she liked to live each day as if it were her last. Mariana in contrast loved to project into the future. One of her dreams was to build a rehabilitation centre for children with cancer and Samantha told her yes, when they got back to Culiacán they would look for a lot to build on and in a year it would be up and running. We'll have Leo McGiver get the equipment in the United States. That is wonderful, truly; on another topic, I think it's time you called your son and then off to your date. You think of everything. Am I not the adviser-in-chief? Will you go with me? No, I'll stick with Sor Juana, and I'm going to call your mother's house to see how Luigi's doing, poor guy, he looked so sad. That dog is like a son to you.

They entered the hotel, which was draped in Christmas lights. She had less than an hour to dress for the part.

A window eased open when they were seen arriving. Most of the attendees were in Hyena Wong's room: calm, confident, amused, they knew the meeting would be over quickly and then on to bigger and better things, since where there's smoke, there's fire.

From his room, feeling fairly nauseous, Ugarte watched the women, then closed his eyes.

Eleven

They were having breakfast at the Miró, huevos à la Leonor, when Mendieta's cell phone rang: it was Trudis. What's the story, Lefty, did you fall out of bed? Work, Trudis, you know how hard we work to make sure everyone can live their lives in safety. You don't say, give that bone to another dog, have you seen the newspaper? eighteen bodies all across the state, more than where the Taliban are; are you coming home for breakfast? Not this time. Are you going to leave young Jason by himself? You have breakfast with him, we're in the middle of an operation. I'd better put him on. Hi. How are you this morning? Fine, you're the ones who were up all night, I got home before Mama. We had a lot to talk about. I thought so, I brought your car back. Do you need it today? If you'll lend it to me, yes. Go ahead, give me your mother's number. She was sleeping when I left. I'll call her in a couple of hours. Remember you owe me a present. So tell me, what do you want? Hmm, I'll tell you later, not on the telephone. Alright, I'll drop by the house in a little while in case you're still there. I was looking at your bookshelf, would you lend me *Under the Volcano*? It's yours. O.K., I'll see you later, we're going to Altata for lunch. With the same girls? Two and two. Be careful, there are a lot of bad guys around there.

Zelda smiled. Boss, are you ever the model policeman, you never give anyone a peek at your private life. Agent Toledo, if you were paying attention, you would know that we have no private life, not you or me or anybody else. If you don't have one now, you must have had one once, I mean if that boy is any indication, what's his name? Jason. Are you going to deny he's your son? Mendieta sipped his coffee, signalled Bety for another cup. I'm not going to deny it, the same as I can't quite accept it, can you believe that I just met him and it was only the other day I learned he existed? Does he have a mother? Of course, last night we reached an agreement, I'm going to provide support so Jason can go to college. That's good. Zelda wanted another orange juice, which Rudy brought immediately. On the sound system, Dolly Parton singing "Winter Wonderland". Last night I told Rodo, before we set a date for the wedding I want him to make sure he doesn't have a child running around somewhere, imagine us happily married and some kid turns up asking to borrow the car. Don't exaggerate, Agent Toledo, I don't think this happens very often. I'd rather he make sure, look, we thought you were practically a saint and here you've got a kid you'd never met, is the mother married? Lefty realised he had not asked, apart from Jason they had not talked about anything else, and yet he had gone ahead and asked Jason for her number so he could invite her to Devil Urquídez's wedding. I don't know. This morning you looked so happy I figured you had something going with somebody. Hey, why does everybody think waking up happy only comes from not sleeping alone? there are lots of reasons to wake up happy. That's true, but nothing compares to a nice night with company, don't deny it, you can even see it in their complexion. Seventh Cavalry Charge: Mendieta. Edgar? Is there another? Well, there's Jason and there's Enrique, you aren't the only one. How are you feeling this morning? A little headachy, but fine, what a phenomenal night. You overdid it with the sambuca. Zelda chewed slowly, enjoying Lefty's amorous banter, in his face you could see the world being reborn every four seconds. Jason told me you wanted to speak to me. Ah, yes, tonight Benito is getting married and there'll be a lamb on a spit and . . . Count me in, is it very formal? Hmm, I don't think so. Will we go to the Mass or just the party? Just the party, I'll pick you up at nine thirty, how does that sound? Perfect, take care. Click. Lefty looked at his partner, who was still smiling. You didn't ask if she was married, eh? Tonight I will. Do you see why I asked Rodo to go over everything? imagine the sucker coming out with some Sunday surprise just because I once gave him a week off. Now Lefty was the one smiling, and at the same time shaking his head in disapproval. Again the Seventh Cavalry Charge. It was Ortega: You bastard, I heard about your son, why didn't you tell me? Well, I'm still waiting on the D.N.A. results. Are you ever fucked up, you must be scared shitless, it even brought back the time we first met; congratulations and forgive me for not being much help with your questions, I'm afraid I don't really know that much, you even got me to thinking; what's more, tonight I'm going to take Memo and my old lady out for hamburgers. Go to McDonald's, so you can go on disability. What makes you think that shit could do anything to me, my stomach is cast iron; listen, we finished the analysis on Dr Manzo: Jack the Ripper everywhere, but the two specks of cocaine are pure, which means it was somebody heavy, maybe with bodyguards, in the bathroom we found several footprints, all sneakers, which is what most of the young hitmen wear, we found splashes of urine on the edge of the bowl and sent samples to the lab, but that's all we're waiting on; they used two calibres, a .45 and a 5.4×28, which I already told you; and we found some outlines of letters on the desk in the waiting room though none of them is clear, it looks like they were writing on a piece of paper with a magic marker and a little seeped through. Another bastard who committed suicide. Listen, if you want to bring your son along we'll be at Tatankas at eight. I'll pass, the kid's going to Altata with a chick. Good sign, he didn't turn out a faggot like you; by the way give him some change for condoms, it shouldn't happen to him what happened to another jerk I know. Your mother, asshole.

The Camel, a short fat officer with a bit of a hump on his back, led Lizzie Tamayo to the interrogation room. His erection was evident. The widow, wearing a black miniskirt and a low-cut white blouse, sashayed along beside him then settled herself in a chair in a way that magnified her charms. Poor is the poor man, heaven knows, he'll be fucked wherever he goes, the badge reflected before calling in the detectives.

How long were you married? Since '96, it's been, what, twelve years? eleven? Lizzie, I can't believe how great you look, how do you do it? how do you keep your weight down? You have to be on it every single day; people say the key to happiness is leading a good life, but that isn't it, the key is looking good; keeping your figure takes sacrifice, nothing easy about it, but is it ever worth it; you can't eat whatever you want or stay up late or overdo anything, you have to stay out of the sun and, well, you need to know which creams are the ones to use during the day and which at night, which perfume to use when, what clothes go with what accessories; don't trust the sunscreens they advertise, they're worthless; you're not bad yourself, eh? You're making that up, Zelda smiled, I look really awful. Don't think like that, a little dieting, an hour's walk every day, abdominals, stretches, remember motion is lotion, and you'll be a beauty queen; first, I'd recommend using a good day cream, get a chic haircut, tell them not too short, don't forget it's December. I'll take your advice. Do it, you're young and you only live once, oh, and drink a lot of water, at least two litres a day, hydration is beautification. Lefty came in. Well, thank you, now to the matter at hand, where were you the night they killed your husband? Lizzie stiffened. At home, I prepared supper and waited for him. What did you cook? Black Forest ham sandwiches with Diet Coke. You sure know how to eat well, what did you do when Dr Manzo didn't come home? First I called his cell, but he didn't answer, at about ten I ate my sandwich and curled up in bed to watch television, I fell asleep and when I woke up it was getting light; I always encouraged him to go out with his friends, I thought he'd finally taken my advice. Who are his friends? Well, he really didn't have any, what I wanted was for him to go out and meet girls, that sort of thing. You aren't the jealous type. Why should I be? you only live once. What time did you learn the truth? At nine the next morning, when Noemí called. You have relations with two people, did they ever threaten him? Never. Did you ever talk about hiring someone to kill him? Never, ever. Did one of them want you all to himself? No, I don't think so, with both of them it's always been clear as could be: have a good time and that's it. Did you go out with anyone else, someone who might be angry enough at your husband to murder him? Of course not, in the beginning I had a fling with my gynaecologist for a couple of months, but he's easygoing; that was about ten years ago. Did your husband tell you about any troublesome patients? The undersecretary of the economy, that was a guy who set his teeth on edge, he was stingy, never wanted to pay; as a matter of fact, his wife is a very good-looking woman who was my classmate at the Tech. But in general, did you two get along? Really well, my girlfriends always said how great he was; yesterday they all kept me company saying goodbye to him. Lefty stepped out of the room, discouraged. A minute later the women went back to diets and other ways of keeping themselves beautiful and attractive. Raise the hemlines of your dresses a bit and keep a tight fit, every man likes to see asses and legs . . .

Edgar Mendieta and Susana Luján, he in his customary attire and she wearing a blue dress, stepped into the Texas Banquet Hall, a favourite of the narcos. It was 10.30 at night and the atmosphere was strangely uneasy. The two bands hired to play were silent and there was a murmur of voices. They went straight to the table set aside for gifts and left a microwave oven, and then over to say hello to Shorty Abitia, the father of the bride, who looked more pot-bellied and insignificant in a suit than in his usual shirt and jeans. He was surrounded by family.

What's up, my man Shorty, how's the fuse? Welcome, my man Lefty, and turning to Susana, How are you? sit with us, can I pour you a bucanitas? Good idea, where's the happy couple? They left twenty minutes ago. Really? they must have left the oven on high. It's not that, my man Lefty, Devil was told to get himself over to the Valdés house, and, well, Begoña is his woman now, so he took her along. Did he say anything about why or what? No, but it must be a huge mess, he seemed really upset; look, with all the shit coming down you never know, soon there'll be more dead bodies than live ones. Poor Devil, he couldn't enjoy his wedding in peace. As long as they don't kill him, I'll be happy. Why isn't anybody dancing? Well, that's why; what, do you feel like shaking off the fleas? Since you mentioned it.

Seven minutes later more than a hundred couples were dancing to "El Son de los Aguacates".

Outside, a military convoy drove slowly by, unnerving Chopper Tarriba and his band of bodyguards keeping watch on the party.

Twelve

Samantha Valdés entered the meeting room at twenty-two minutes past eight; everyone stood up. Enclosed space, meticulously inspected for recording or broadcasting devices. She looked relaxed. Beside the long table with its nine cushioned chairs were two small ones that held drinks and snacks people could take as they wished; a vase of fragrant roses sat on each. Ugarte had before him a half-full glass of water with ice and a bit of Coke so it looked like a Cuba Libre; he had served himself a cracker with cheese, though he did not eat it, and had placed himself at the far end of the table, away from Samantha, who sat at the head. Fewer of the attendees would see him face-to-face. Pallid, but exhilarated, feeling the usual slight nausea, he kept his focus. Max Garcés stood guard.

The first thing I'll say is that we have to remain united, La Jefa declared as she accepted a Buchanan's with ice and mineral water. Our enterprise is a business, not a criminal syndicate. Day in, day out, the President keeps insisting this is a war and quite a few have taken the bait; we will not. He's the one who is vulnerable, not us. I know for a fact, because it's already happened to two of you, that every single one of you will receive invitations to ally with other organisations. Let's not do that. The small fry are getting wiped out, they don't see the trap until after they've fallen in; if they allow themselves to be fooled that's their business. I invited the heads of the other groups, and you can see that none of them was interested, they'd rather have their guts cut out than try to forge an alliance. In our case, the business comes first, our clients, our routes. Politicians are always going to be grandstanding, the point is to keep them from acting on it. The United States isn't going to decriminalise, even if their president claims that's where he's headed. At least that's what my informants tell me, two of them are here today, and as long as that doesn't happen, we have our market guaranteed. And the market rules. The gringos nodded in approval.

But, señora, what are we going to do? nearly two dozen of my boys have been killed. We'll hire more, there are about fifteen million to choose from, and you're going to make sure none of them is on the make and none of them picks any fights; explain to them that this is the way we run our business.

What do we do about the routes that have been disrupted? We win them back; of course, if we can't do that nicely, then we'll get nasty: the ends justify the means.

Señora, on my route they want more money. Tell them yes, we're negotiating with the guys on top; what's essential is that they see we are united, division would weaken us; has anyone had trouble obtaining weapons?

In my case it's getting easier and easier, they're sold like any other contraband.

For me too; I get offers every day, and at good prices.

Does anyone have any doubts about who our main enemies are?

They all shook their heads.

Chávez, in Juárez can we share the territory?

That's my boss's proposal, we're expecting a meeting with the bros.

Tijuana then, did the politician who wanted more money simmer down?

Everything is settled, señora, Ugarte directed his answer at the figure in the pistachio-green dress and matching earrings.

What about La Paz?

We have no problems at all, in fact we're investing in several sectors of the economy and we've created new sources of employment.

That's important, we've got to help the people, they should have places to work besides directly in our operations.

Somebody from *Forbes* magazine wants to talk to you, what should I say? they want to put you on the list of the world's billionaires.

A little more than half an hour later the meeting was over. She shook everyone's hand and left the room. The representatives did the same. Another twenty minutes and none of them remained in the hotel. Days later, at a crucial moment, Ugarte would recall her firm handshake and intense gaze: Say hello to your boss, tell him to send you more often, we prefer lieutenants who are good-looking and more prudent than the Hunk. With pleasure, I shall tell him, señora.

From her room Samantha called her son again. They had spoken for nearly an hour before the meeting and she had not managed to calm him down; she had to promise she would pick him up the next day in Pasadena, California, where she had sent him for safe-keeping and he was attending a bilingual school. Of course they would not spend Christmas vacation apart. César was a demanding child, and there was little she could say, since the boy was right.

Honey, are you feeling any better? Mama, I mean it, I want to be with you, like I told you, I'm the only child in the world who's been left alone. Of course, my love, I'll be there tomorrow, but in the meantime I don't want you to be sad, your whole life lies ahead of you, lots of opportunities for us to be together. Christmas is special, Mama, and it only comes once a year. She hesitated: What's with this kid, who got him so worked up? But who said we wouldn't be together? we'll be there tomorrow, meanwhile think about what you'd like to do. Aren't we going to Culiacán? because I want to see Grandma. I'm trying to convince her to come with us, if I need your help I'll call you; I wanted to surprise you, but you're too smart for me. Mama, I love you. I love you too, my prince, now you dream about the angels because tomorrow we'll have lots to do, shall we go to Disneyland? Oh, I'd rather go out for hamburgers, are you coming in our plane? Of course, in case you feel like going somewhere else. Except for Culiacán, right? If we're all with you, what do you want to come to Culichi for? To see the pictures of bodies in the newspapers, they're really cool. Oof, well, we'll decide when we get there, after all we'll have the plane on hand. Bring shrimp. Wow, my love, so small and already nostalgic about so many things. And Guacamaya sauce. We'll bring everything, don't worry, now go to sleep. I love you, Mama. And I love you.

She sat thinking for a moment. No way around it, she also had to be a mother. The next day they would have to leave early for Culiacán and then on to Pasadena. She stood up, she would tell Mariana right away and then call her mother so she could get ready. They would be happy to see César. He's so little, but every day he's more like his grandfather, maybe he'll grow up to be like him; but for the moment the one who needs to keep people in line is me, the meeting did not go badly, I just hope none of them gets any bright ideas. Mariana must be deep into a book or watching television, she's crazy about that Monica Lavín; that's why it's so quiet in there, and she's fascinated by Sor Juana just because she was one of us. She opened the door, television on, Mariana in a bathrobe, asleep face down, her thighs uncovered. Lights turned low. Book on the dresser. At a glance she knew something was not right. Hmm. She might have fallen asleep in her old blue bathrobe at home, but in a hotel? She moved closer, touched her hand: cold. Oh, hair wet, she turned her fragile body over. Bullet-hole in her forehead. My God. They say the good thing about women is that they cry, but Samantha froze and could only stare. What did they do to you, honey? She fell to her knees and put her head on Mariana's breast. She was trembling. Eyes dry, but shining. Pretty Mama, what did they do to you? Fuck it all. She closed her eyes for a few seconds. Whoa. Then she rose and walked slowly out of the room.

She would have bitten down on her balls, but how do you chew on an ovary?

Thirteen

Motel.

She stood still: barefoot, ardent, quivering. Man with a three-day beard, so nervous she had trouble getting him to let go, was drinking her in. She fixated on his eyes. Brown. She thought about taking his clothes off piece by piece, about caressing him bit by bit, but that was not her nature. She dropped to her knees, unzipped his black jeans, pulled out his sizable member, and wrapped her mouth around it. Mmmm. She sucked him avidly. Cherry Popsicle, but warm. The man grabbed her head, moaned softly, but she only heard the keening of his body, the total eclipse of the heart. He resisted: I'm not going to come like a school-kid, nope. His body cheered him on: Buddy, let's go, you wanted action? get to it, apply yourself, you bastard. He quickly rid himself of his clothes and steered her to the bed, raised her skirt and went straight to the apple, the one that really got caught in Adam's throat. A large mole on her dark pubis. A place of rest. Her excitement grew, her entire being lay in her crotch, and she licked her lips, umm, yum, ahhh. He nibbled at her clitoris, at her large pink labia, and the woman teetered from spasm to spasm. Aghh. His hands on her compact tits. Aaghh. Convulsive orgasm. She pulled him toward her while turning to offer him her round ass, and he penetrated her to the hilt. Ahhh. He watched her magnificent behind coming and going, coming and going, and caressed her back which felt strong in that moment when no-one is fragile. I'm not going to come, not yet, no. He pulled it out, she turned to face him. Come inside me. He licked her nipples, her neck, he kissed her pillowy lips. Come inside as far as you can; she put her legs on his shoulders and he penetrated her anew. She took him defiantly. Ahhh. She rubbed his nipples, licked his hands, his wrists and gave herself over to the cock that was stroking her stoking her screwing her skewering her. Make me come. He thrust and thrust and in a few minutes she convulsed anew. Aaaghh. Then he ejaculated. Oghh. She pumped her hips against him. Ohhh, the only high in the world that's worth the effort.

Motel.

Fourteen

The Secretary was holding a glass of whisky with ice when he heard the ring of the cell phone whose number he had given Ugarte. A variety of toy giraffes on the desk. He turned to face the large window filled with city lights. Tell me. We finished ten minutes ago. Are you still on the scene? We all left immediately, here is the information. He relayed every word: the certainties, the doubts and the promises. Nine, and all of them from the Pacific Cartel, no-one else. That's all? Precisely. Do you know the name of the politician in Tijuana? Same as yours. Is the señora good-looking? Very good-looking. What about her body? Perfect. They tell me she dresses very formally, likes dark colours. Something like that. How will you leave the city, Señor Ugarte? By sea, señor. In case you'd like to know, what you have reported is a piece of shit, it's worthless, not even that bit about her thinking we're vulnerable; this is more proof of how ludicrous your reputation is. He interrupted: Well, Señor Secretary, it was a pleasure working with you, good luck. He pitched the cell out of his car window on to the highway so with any luck it would get crushed by the tyre of some rented V.W. Crunch. He felt tense, persecuted, no reason I have to listen to his threats; a sharp pain in his abdomen, nausea. Mediocre jerk. His discomfort worsened, I think I overdid it, everything hurts. He pulled over to the side of the road, would he use his pistol? He opened the door and vomited into the darkness. It was a sign of one day fewer and one activity too many. Not in that open field. A black car raced past. He thought about his wife María, about his daughter Francelia and his son Aramís, who was so far away. He vomited again. To be sick is to be doubly alone.

A searchlight from the Mazatlán airport illuminated him for a moment, then he closed the door and drove on, which of the men at the meeting did he recognise? Two; of those, only one scrutinised him at any length. He turned on the radio: "Bethlehem, bells of Bethlehem that the angels ring, what good news for us do you bring..."

Fifteen

Max Garcés escorted the gunslinger in charge of watching Mariana's room toward the golf course. The young man was bathed in sweat. He knew he was going to die, who could save him? No-one. Eight metres behind, two bodyguards followed. Not even the fact that he was a relative of the señora's. His last hopes evaporated in the cold onshore breeze. Both were wearing black hats. They stopped. If you're straight with me, we'll protect your family, if you aren't you know perfectly well what we'll do: tell me what you saw, what you heard, what you smelled. Nothing, boss, no-one came near, only a few gringos coming back from the beach besides our guys doing the rounds, who would come by every so often. Use your memory, asshole. Nothing, truly, the gringos were all sandy and drunk, all of them. Did you see the Bogeyman or any of the others? Nobody, just the guys doing the rounds. Did the Bogeyman say anything to you? We never spoke, those are the orders you gave us: him inside and me outside. The hotel has a video of everything that happens in that hallway twenty-four hours a day, but I want you to tell me. I never went in, boss, I swear by Malverde, by my children, by the Virgin of Guadalupe, but if you've got to kill me, go ahead, I'm happy to be in this world, but if my number's up, just do it. Garcés studied him. How much did they pay you to play the dummy? Treason never, boss, that isn't my way, if you don't want to kill me, then I'll kill myself, but I would never betray the Valdés family. Garcés studied him again, calmer; his father and brothers had died serving Don Marcelo Valdés, Samantha's father. Unless you were the one. Not even if God willed it, boss, truly; I'm a man and I would never do anything like that, and if you aren't convinced, go ahead and kill me and my family, I'm a man loyal unto death and if I have to prove it, bring it on; besides, you know better than I, she was really nice, I haven't forgotten how she sent a present when my son was born. Garcés breathed in, patted Drysnot on the back, and decided to let him live; the video showed the hallway empty of strangers, except for an elderly couple on canes, and it was humanly impossible to get in by the window without being seen. Who killed her and how did he reach her? Garcés realised the matter was beyond him. That is what he told Samantha Valdés minutes later in her room.

I can't believe we are surrounded by such dolts, how could it be? Max, I asked you to get me the best, you said they were the best, and then this? Señora, I can't explain it either.

What do you think Marcelo Valdés would have done if they'd killed my mother?

Max Garcés had not thought about it like that, but he knew that was not the answer to give. He remained silent for a few seconds.

We'll do something, señora.

Answer me, asshole, what would my father have done?

Señora, I don't know, your father was special.

He would get even, Max, he would make sure his vengeance was as bloody as possible and that is precisely what we are going to do; someone had the balls to do it, and now many are going to pay the price; if they think they're going to cow me with this murder, they are fools; if you don't know where to start, then with pleasure I will tell you.

Leave it to me.

Well, do something in Mazatlán, so they know Samantha Valdés only plays hardball.

She took a slug from the bottle of whisky then smashed it on the floor, even though it was nearly full. No more alcohol, she was in the room adjoining the one where the crime took place, where Mariana Kelly's body still lay. I shouldn't be drunk on top of this tragedy weighing on me. Samantha's face turned to stone, she stood and looked over at the window. They say God knows why He does things, but not this time, how could it happen to the nicest woman in the world? she had plans for good works, as if we were politicians; what assholes, I have to phone my mother, and César, poor kid.

Excuse me, señora.

Call Devil, so he can get the funeral home people from San Chelín and tell him to come with them.

He must be at his wedding.

Ask him to do me that favour.

She went to the window and the scenery looked like shit. Fucking tears.

92

Sixteen

Enrique told me you almost died. Sometimes, when too many bullets are flying, a few of them have your name on them.

It was a bit more sensational, like your car exploded, something like that. Don't pay any attention to him, he was always a big talker.

You look really good, I thought you'd be pot-bellied and wrinkled. The one who's incredible is you; truly, you look fantastic.

You imagined me a fat-cheeked lady with her hair dyed yellow and her saggy ass bulging? More or less.

You're horrible. No, I'm not, how could you say that?

I'd think of you every so often, you were that gentle kid who only opened his mouth when he had to and always gave strange answers. And you were a rocket.

I knew how to have a good time, I tried to feel everything, to experience everything, to dream everything.

Girls always pretend to be older; when does a woman stop wanting to celebrate her birthday?

It depends, some women do everything they can to hide their age, even when they're young; they add to their asses, their breasts, they have their faces done, despite the fact that for a number of years we don't change, say between twenty-five and thirty-two; why didn't you get married?

Maybe because I never found the right woman, or she walked

93

right by me and I didn't notice, or because getting drunk seemed preferable to looking for a mate; what about you?

I met at least three people I could have made a life with, but I didn't go through with it, for Jason's sake; all three made some comment about him that scared me off; the last one, for example: what about the kid, can he handle school or is he just a road-runner? That set alarm bells ringing and I backed out.

I didn't get that close, well, maybe once, but she was married and it didn't end well.

They caught you with your hand in the cookie jar.

Worse, they turned out to be murderers and I nearly got caught in their trap.

Really? Did you put them in prison?

Even more drastic, but tell me what you do over there.

I partnered with a friend and we started a taco business, the best tacos in Santa Monica, we're near Hollywood. Do gringos like tacos?

Not the gringos, but for the chicanos they're like catnip, some-times we sell out; the most popular are the political tacos. What's with that name?

They're made with tongue. Seriously? and now that we're speaking frankly, what's your secret for managing to stay so young-looking?

I made a pact with the devil. With Devil Urquídez?

Who's that? The groom of the wedding we just went to.

Why weren't they there? is that the new thing? Not that I know of; in Devil's case, his father-in-law didn't know and he didn't care either, he got his daughter hitched and that was enough to satisfy him.

That never changes, and in the United States it's the same story, despite the fact that kids leave home as soon as they can. Does Jason live his life alone?

He never talks about it, I think he considers himself the man of the house; this afternoon, when he came back from Altata, Mama said a few things about you, that I shouldn't go out with you, that you were dangerous and untrustworthy, and what's more, an alcoholic, and Jason cut her short; he went over and hugged her and whispered that he loved her a lot, but she shouldn't say such things about his father either to his face or behind his back; my mother was left with her mouth hanging open; all she could do was hug him back.

I trust he doesn't do drugs. He was never an addict, but he experimented; now he's managing to steer clear of all that.

Why is he always texting? His friends are the same way, it's the latest fashion; listen, I'm a mother and I've got to get home early; Jason won't go to bed until I turn up.

I hope there's a comfy chair at Doña Mary's.

Seventeen

Ugarte answered his cell. How are you? all night long I was waiting for your call. Good morning, General, the thing was delayed a couple of hours, more, and I thought it would be too late for you. Did everything go according to plan? Just the way you like it. It's a relief to hear that. Last night I called the Secretary, I told him what they talked about and, well, mission accomplished. Now, tell me. The señora's good, clearly in charge, she asked them to remain united, not to send their people out to die in vain, that their business isn't killing but trafficking; she asked each of us about our territories and the meeting was adjourned. Just like her father, right to the point. That seems to be her style. How did the group seem? Tight; however, if she was asking for unity there must be something going on. Do you think that was a threat? Hmm, I couldn't swear to it, it felt more like a preventive measure, it's her feminine nature. Were the kingpins there or just their representatives? Mostly representatives and everyone kept a low profile, there were only people from the Pacific Cartel. Did the Secretary ask you any class-A questions? None, he wanted an interpretation and you know that isn't my thing. That's his job; did he try to humiliate you again? You could say that, he said the information was worthless and denied they were vulnerable, which is a point the señora touched on in the meeting. Perfect, I'll call the President to give him our version, and I'll be seeing you. I'll be expecting a visit.

Are you going to stay there for a while? No, I'll soon be on my way to my own little hell. It's good to spend Christmas with the family; by the way, I just sent you some decorations for your tree that will knock your socks off, people in Yucatan are really ingenious, have you had breakfast? That's what I'm up to now. Me too, enjoy it.

He was flat on his back, pale, no appetite, trembling. He had done his job beyond well, he felt satisfied, but he knew that was it for him. The General was a machine and he demanded the same of his team, but no way could he run around like that anymore, pain was a very effective messenger and all day and night he had felt death at hand. To die, to kill, to be dying, right then it was all the same to him. He reached for his medicine on top of the dresser and turned on the television with the remote. The morning news: Horrifying night, the on-screen journalist said gravely. Last night Mazatlán was bathed in blood, six bodies were found hanging from a bridge and more turned up in various parts of the city peppered with bullets, among them two minors; officials in the port admit they've never seen the city so red in December, despite the fact that it's one of the traditional colours of Christmas. Ugarte flicked it off, who wants to know that? how could it possibly help me? He got out of bed, in pyjamas you could see how much weight he had lost; he took his pistol from the dresser top and put it away in a drawer. In the dust-covered kitchen he drank a can of orange juice, then dialled from the landline. How is the prettiest girl in Cuernavaca? Papa, where are you? my friends all want to meet you. In no man's land, where else? Can you bring us shrimp? Of course, let me talk to your mother. She's in Mexico City, she went yesterday afternoon to see her friends. For her traditional end-of-year supper? *Yes*, in English, I helped her wrap her present. Tell her I get in tonight. Don't forget the shrimp. Bye. Bye-bye. Through the window he saw the street, his front garden full of weeds, the low rusty wrought-iron fence, not a single Christmas decoration. If the General wants to get rid of the Secretary or change anything else, he'll have to do it without me.

Then he went into the bathroom to throw up the juice.

He looked in the mirror, thought hard and decided he'd had an unusual life, he'd done a good job at work, left few promises unkept; but when he tried to accept that he was ready to go, some deep-seated fear stopped him; he refused to admit that the end comes when your number is up. He contemplated his reflection for another moment and that was when he saw it: a shadow behind him, fleeting but unmistakable. Oh.

Eighteen

Dr Uriel Castro Arellano rushed out of his office across from the airport at the Bachigualato city limits. He was fleeing. A few minutes earlier, his assistant had received a call from someone who insisted he make a house call and threatened to come get her and the dentist and drag them both out by the balls if they refused. I do not have balls, sir. But he does and if he doesn't pull my boss's tooth, he'll never hear the end of it in his entire fucking life. Arellano had heard about two murdered dentists and he did not want to become the third. The assistant, who ran out after him, wisely chose to go in the opposite direction; she found a taxi and took refuge at her house about twenty minutes away.

In his haste, the dentist had not removed his white coat. He was striding along so frightened and wild-eyed he did not realise that Uncle Beto and a hired gun were waiting for him at the kerb about thirty metres away, next to a pickup with a door sporting a few visible punctures. A young woman wearing a tight skirt high above her strong thighs, who had an appointment in five minutes, was startled to see the man, usually so calm and respectful, so comfortable in his skin, evidently discombobulated. She pulled out her ear buds playing "My Name is Luka" by Luka Kovač. Eyeglasses are no mask for fear. The young woman, who was studying psychology and working on a thesis about the effects of violence, jumped to the worst conclusion and she was right. In a flash she spotted the gunslingers and decided to intervene. Hey, doctor, what are you doing out here? The appointment has been cancelled, Claudia, his voice came out in a plaintive whine, so unlike the usual suave resonance she found so reassuring when it hurt. Without a thought to the consequences she embraced him and tried to kiss him on the mouth; Arellano pushed her away. Please, don't do that, what's wrong with you? Let me, doctor, I know about the murdered dentists and behind me are two guys waiting for you, kiss me and look at them. But, but. The girl latched on to that dry bloodless mouth smelling of death. The dentist spied Uncle Beto stroking his chin and the hit man staring. He pissed himself. The girl leaned into the closest wall without interrupting her kiss. Grab my ass with all the lust you can muster, so they can't see me using my cell, don't let me go until they come for us. He hugged her timidly. Doctor, make sure they can see my underwear, do it or they'll kill us both right now. He obeyed. The few passers-by slowed their pace, wowed by the girl's behind and a nearly non-existent red thong. The killers approached, they could kidnap the two of them, who was going to stop them? Besides, every dentist needs an assistant.

A patrol car, tooting a blast on its siren, pulled over. The couple stopped kissing, the smirking pedestrians dispersed, the policemen were staggered by the young woman's beauty: Some bastards have more luck than they deserve, partner, don't you agree? Uncle Beto took his crony's arm and moved off. At that moment a green car driven by a woman with long curly hair pulled up. Claudia opened the back door, pushed the dentist in and got in after him. Mama, floor it, take the airport highway, there'll be Federal Police there. What's wrong, child, what's wrong with the dentist? He doesn't feel well. She saw the gunslingers getting into their pickup, but not pulling out behind them. Arellano began to sob. A moment later the women were sobbing too.

Arellano, who hated all police, did not want to lodge a complaint. The girl had interviewed Captain Pineda a number of times; she called him, but he wasn't interested. However, he promised he would take up the case if she would have supper with him. She liked her dentist, but not that much.

Nineteen

Zelda Toledo came in with her Diet Coke and a coffee for Lefty, who was flipping through the newspaper. Any important gossip? Look at this, a half-page photograph of the Urquídez–Abitia wedding. Don't they look nice! her dress I like, her make-up is perfect, they're your friends, right? Sure, Devil used to work with us. He looks happy, did you go to the wedding? For a little while. Because I can see you're looking happy too, eh? The past few days I've slept well. I suppose you have. Is there something wrong, Agent Toledo? Nothing, boss, nothing at all, but you should know that in womanly matters, we women always see more than meets the eye, and of course in many other matters too. Lefty turned to the crime page: "Six Found Hanging from Bridge in Mazatlán", above a photograph of the bodies swinging like piñatas from a pedestrian overpass. Will you look at that, boss, demons are on the loose in Mazatlán. Plus twenty-three shot and four Hummers set on fire. Noriega must be going nuts. I don't think so, my buddy is probably just the way he always is, enjoying life with plenty of beer and aguachile; and for sure he knows who's behind all this. The cartels, boss, who else? It could be they're members of some religious sect and they all committed suicide. You don't say. Angelita from the doorway: Good morning, Zelda, zero, no calls; boss, the commander wants to see you. We've run aground on Manzo, haven't we? Oh, it's not that, Zelda wants to know if anyone's called you. Angelita! Me? what for?

Then Zelda confessed: We only want to know who the lucky woman in your life might be. I forbid you to stick your noses into my affairs, who do you think you are? jeez, it's hard to believe, have I ever disrespected you or got involved in your personal life? Pardon me, boss, I just wanted to . . . Well, don't want to! He sauntered out toward Briseño's office, he was smiling.

The commander was eating wholewheat bread with his coffee. Chief, are you on a diet? Me? that would be the last mistake I'd make, man was born to eat, everything else is an accident. My, oh my, commander, you're wearing your thinking cap today, aren't you? congratulations. What I can't see anywhere is yours, he threw a centimetre-thick folder at him; what did you do to Constantino Blake Hernández? take a look at the recommendations the National Human Rights Commission sent us. We interrogated him the usual way. Let your grandma believe that one, his brother is practically asking for my head, he complains about torture, discrimination and obstruction in calling his lawyer. Seriously? What's wrong with you, Edgar? in every single case you stir up trouble; do your job by the book and save me the bother of scolding you as if you were a rookie. Chief, I'm not lying, we didn't touch a hair on the guy's head, even though he's an arrogant sonofabitch and was sneering at us the whole time and treating us like we were idiots. Look at the pictures, you nearly killed him; no wonder Gori seemed so intense over there; give me the report on what happened and read that tome, I've got to send some sort of answer. Tell him his brother's a jerk. The jerk is you, and it's occurring to me that I should hold you responsible for what happened; you could spend a couple of years behind bars. Only a couple? if you come visit me, bring some of that bread, it looks delicious. By the way, what happened to Quiroz? because I haven't seen him for the longest time. No idea, maybe he's one of the journalists who passed on to a better life. Jesus, are you serious? We really don't know, maybe the Martians took him. Well, I want a report on what you've got on Blake. What I told you: a dentist was murdered, Blake was or is the widow's lover and he doesn't want to say where he was the night of the crime. Name of the dentist? I already told you that too, Humberto Manzo Solís. For a minute there I thought it was the one I go to, who's leading me down a bitter path. You weren't so lucky; alright, I'll look at this. And hurry up with the report, I need something so I can defend myself; listen, you look different, refreshed, like you're at a good point in your life. Your diet's gone to your head, chief, I'm the same. You even have more colour in your cheeks. He left without answering.

Mendieta felt uneasy as he made his way back to his office and his mood dipped further when he looked at the pictures in the report from the National Human Rights Commission: various body parts bruised and swollen and three all bloody; what's more, a vitriolic rant on the tortures inflicted by police outside the capital, especially in Culiacán, where the photographs were from, whose force stood out for its savagery and cruelty. The report demanded an explanation and recommended handing those implicated over to a federal authority to establish culpability. Wow. Agent Toledo, did they do something to Blake I don't know about? How could you think that, boss, we didn't touch him, not even with a rose petal, despite how unbearable he was. Well, we're deep in shit, look at these pictures. Zelda contemplated them in silence; when she looked up, she said: The guy wants to screw us. Find Ortega, get him to figure out who these people in the pictures are; and tell Gori to meet us here this evening at seven.

Mendieta called Jason but could not reach him, and Susana was out with friends. He went home and found Trudis cooking and singing: "Sometimes you remind me of someone . . ." I can hardly believe it, but I'm so happy you're here. What happened? Well, practically nothing, young Jason wants to eat pescado zarandeado and I'm making it for him. Is he here? He went out to the Oxxo for some pop and the fish is turning out perfect, so don't start telling me you've got an emergency, you'll stay here to eat with your son and if you want to invite Susana go ahead and bring her over, there's enough for everyone; listen to me, isn't she the looker? wow, the years don't go by for that woman, and what a body. I don't know anything. Don't play the dummy, the whole block is talking about how many nights in a row you two have gone out. Really? Do you think this is a rich neighbourhood where word doesn't get around as soon as things happen? not here, no, señor, here everybody knows everything and, by the way, they say there's a gringo driving around in a black pickup who won't leave her in peace. Mendieta stiffened. That gringo, did he come with her from California? No, people are saying he turned up asking for Doña Mary and then for Susana, hasn't she told you about it? Have you asked Jason? What are you thinking, not even if God willed it, what I want is for that boy to feel at home, I'm not going to start asking him about his mother. They heard the Jetta parking in the street behind the Toyota. As you can see, he's not going to miss my zarandeado, I put in a bit of green mustard and all three onions, purple, white and yellow, plus green pepper and fresh celery; it's coming out of the oven. Now I'm hungry.

Lefty opened the door. Jason texted on his cell, put it away and stepped in carrying a supermarket bag. How was Altata? Great, it was Gustavo, my cousin who wants to kill himself, plus his girlfriend, another girl and me. He wants to kill himself? Yeah, but in his car, he drives like a maniac, that's why I asked for yours; I think what he wants is to get his father's attention. Who's his father? My Uncle Domingo, he's a colonel in the army, he's never lived with Aunt Aracely, but he's always supported them. O.K., so you enjoyed the beach. We had a good time: we ate, we went for a banana-boat ride and we swam a bit. As cold as it is? It was cool, but a lot of people were in the water; California's where the water's really cold, practically ice, and still people go in. The highway wasn't too bad? More Hummers and Cheyennes than on a Los Angeles freeway at five in the afternoon. The bros love them. My cousin says they're the narcos' favourites. That's true, and besides liking them they can afford them; so we're going to eat zarandeado? Trudis is promising glory, listen I brought in the C.D.s I gave you, I see you haven't listened to them. Remember, we traded cars, I haven't had a chance. If you like, we can trade again, that Toyota is a dream. You stay in the Jetta and don't knock it, it's a piece of history. Of course I won't, besides, the speakers are awesome, I can tell you listen to music all the time; which one should I put on? Mendieta glanced at the C.D.

box, on the cover the thick letters that spelled out Dylan's name were filled with pictures of him, Clapton, Wonder, Young, Harrison, Petty, McGuinn and two he couldn't identify. Number two looks good. Jason worked the stereo under Lefty's watchful gaze; the young man looked up: As you can see, I'm right-handed. How original. They smiled. Gentlemen, the fish is served.

Basic ways to eat an oven-grilled zarandeado, which should be golden-brown and placed at the centre of the table:

A. Put one serving on each diner's plate and give them utensils.

B. As tacos. Serve directly into corn tortillas and eat as is or with a bit of mayonnaise either dolloped on top or spread on the tortilla before putting in the fish.

C. Serve with wholegrain bread, preferably a flatbread, so the full flavour of the fish comes through.

Hot sauce to taste.

They had tamarind juice from a bottle, but the dish goes well with any good-quality red wine, preferably a shiraz, or a good light beer.

"Just Like Tom Thumb's Blues" with Neil Young on the stereo. The Santa Clauses were vibrating. From a short distance, Trudis observed them with a motherly smile. If I weren't looking at how much you two look alike I wouldn't believe it: like two drops of water. "The Seventh Cavalry Charge" broke in. Mendieta. Boss, Gori doesn't want to see you, he's really depressed. What? Yup, I'm at his house, he even wants to resign. Put him on. What's up, my man Lefty? Nothing, my friend Gori, what about you, what fart are you holding back? Oh, I feel kind of ashamed, Zelda told me you want to see me, but I'm just not up to it. Are you sure? Absolutely sure. What about tomorrow? Tomorrow will be another day, my man Lefty. O.K., put Zelda back on. Go ahead, boss. This is the first I've ever heard of a badge in his specialty getting depressed. He looks sad and he hasn't even showered. What do you think? Well, boss, I think we should leave him alone, maybe tomorrow he'll feel better. Alright, tell him I'll stop by for him tomorrow. Even though it's Sunday? We can't leave a key member of the team with his self-esteem on the floor until Monday.

He told Jason about it.

That Blake, is he a tall, strong, good-looking guy? You know him? He was at the restaurant in Altata boasting about how he gave a badge what was coming. Who was he telling? Gustavo, the owner and two friends, I understood he has a house there, do you want me to find it? No, we'll see him on Monday, but you say he was bragging? The nicest thing he said was they couldn't hold him and he was going to give them the fright of their lives. Trudis brought out dessert: ate de membrillo with cheese from Chihuahua and hot water for Nescafé. Jason kissed her on the cheek: you are the best cook in the world, Trudis. Oh, young Jason, you give me goosebumps. The boy's cell rang. Yup, I'm with Edgar; O.K., he stood up; Mama isn't feeling well, I'm going to Grandma's house and I'll let you know how she is. Wait, I just called her, your grandmother told me she was out with friends. She did? well, she hasn't been out all day. If you wouldn't mind, I'd like to go with you. Jason thought about it. Wait here, I'll call you. He tasted the dessert and raced out. Lefty turned to Trudis, his eyebrows raised. You'd better go, Lefty, after all, you're already involved.

In the air, Bob Dylan sang on: "It's Alright Ma (I'm Only Bleeding)".

Twenty

Overcast. Mariana Kelly's funeral, just like her wake and open-casket Mass, was private with no fanfare. Humaya Gardens at noon, the Valdés family mausoleum. Not even the kingpins were told to attend; travelling turned out to be complicated and better not to risk any surprises. Many were those who dreamed of catching them all in the same place. Mariana's family understood and went along with the arrangements, since she was someone they saw little of and whose friends and lifestyle they did not share. But a goodbye is a goodbye.

The funeral unfolded at its own unhurried pace. Flowers, embraces, prayers. Then a norteño band sang "Te Vas, Ángel Mío" and quickly departed.

Garcés had people all over the cemetery and the family travelled relatively undisturbed in armoured cars.

Devil Urquídez did not have time for his honeymoon; in fact he was not even thinking about it, busy as he was shooting his A.K.-47 all over the state and all through the day and night. People were being murdered in every part of the country except Mexico City, which they chose to respect. Samantha Valdés wanted to make sure that everyone who needed to understood just how upset she was and how ferocious she could be: Make it crystal clear to those bastards. Max Garcés looked into who might be behind the crime and got nowhere; he expected to be asked at any moment and he had to have an answer; after all he felt responsible, his security plan had failed, and had it ever.

Two days later Samantha received a few polite calls and visits. She asked them not to leave their territories and not to panic either, saying that everything would come out in the wash, but from that moment on only the kingpins themselves would meet, no more lieutenants. I never thought all those bodies were ours, most of them said, and they offered their support. When Hunk Gómez found out what had happened, he could not quite put it all together. He had been awakened the day after by his bodyguards, bereft of money and women, and it did not take him long to figure out he had missed the meeting. What a dimwit you are, he railed at the fat one, since someone had to be held responsible. He tried not to make any ripples, and a few hours after his return to Tijuana the matter was forgotten. Now he thought he had better mention it to his boss as soon as the man got back from Las Vegas, where at that moment he was busy was losing several thousand dollars.

While her people wreaked havoc, Samantha Valdés closeted herself in the mansion in Lomas de San Miguel, her mother and son at her side. She cursed, she cried, she threatened; her mother attempted to distract her and console her with advice: Only the boss knows the load he carries and some days that load is hard to bear, but that's why he's the boss: to be tough, to know how to suffer in silence and never to waver in his decisions. That's the way my father was, wasn't he? If men like him aspired to political office, my husband would have been president. Imagine that, you would have been the first lady. Nonsense, there are things that are not for the likes of us; and you, my daughter, how long are you going to go on with these killings? Until it's enough. Minerva observed her for a few seconds, then gave her a hug: No more, please, I'm begging you; and if no-one in Culiacán dies, all the better; however you look at it, in the end we're all neighbours. Samantha took comfort in her arms, wanted to accede to her plea, but still did not feel sated. She whimpered: I promise, Mama. Minerva made her look into her eyes. In memory of your father? She nodded and continued crying. Lying in the garden beside a tree filled with Christmas balls, Luigi waited.

That night the toll rose by another twenty-seven and counting.

Twenty-One

The black pickup with California plates was parked across from the house of Doña Mary, the widow Luján. When Lefty spotted it ahead he kept walking, but he felt a slight chill in the pit of his stomach: Does this concern me, or am I one of those idiots who thinks he has rights over a woman the moment she opens her legs to him? Well, we have a son together and we've had a good time, even so I'd better call Jason, she said he acted like the head of the family. You want to go, don't play the dummy, curiosity is going to kill you. Hang on . . . Stop going in circles, Lefty, the chick is hot and she's eager. Who the fuck asked you to stick your nose in? Me, I'm your body, asshole, and I haven't been so lovingly caressed in a very long time. So don't mess with me. You don't expect us to share her with that faggot from the pickup, do you? Silence. Aha, that shut your trap, didn't it, fucking Lefty? Come on, let me think, let's find out what shit that bro is up to and then we'll see. But his rumination continued: What am I after? do I want to be her Kleenex? maybe she's laying a trap and here I go with my innocent mug and fall right into it? "Lady, look at what your love has made of me." He spied the Jetta parked across from the pickup, and the idea of turning back took hold of him. He slowed his steps. Maybe they're having a heart-to-heart, they've reached some agreement, they're going to start a new family, why should I show my face? He was fifty metres away when he heard a gunshot and it came from the house. Shit, he started trotting and, go figure, he did not have his pistol with him; he expected the neighbours to come out, but no-one did, maybe they thought it was fireworks; it was the right time of year. At the gate he could hear women crying. He tore up the garden path, found the front door ajar and opened it the way police do, with a kick. Jason turned to look at him, as did Susana, Doña Mary, two children including the one that had opened the door for him the first night, plus a boy Jason's age, and of course a tall, brawny gringo with tattoos on his arms. He was wearing a tight T-shirt. Ooh-la-la.

Shouts of Edgar, hey, aha, oh-oh, whoa; and the glassy stare of the gringo whose name could not possibly be Arnold Schwarzenegger, but damned if he didn't look like him.

Jason was pointing a nickel-plated revolver at Arnold.

Susana Luján was wearing white, like Susana San Juan in *Pedro Páramo*, and looking just as pale.

Lefty, his balls in his throat, stared at them for a long moment right out of Salvador Elizondo's *Farabeuf*. "April Come She Will" by Simon & Garfunkel crossed his mind, why? no idea, "The Boxer" would have made more sense. What's going on? This man has been stalking my mother, Jason said coldly; he harasses her at her work, at our house in Pasadena, and as if that weren't enough he followed us all the way here. No-one seemed to be wounded. Mendieta felt an urge to order, Shoot the fucking jerk in the head, but what he said was: Put down the gun. I can explain, Susana blurted out, all jittery but still looking as though she had been painted by Velázquez. You explain nothing, Schwarzenegger barked, his

114

breath stinking of alcohol, this is my business, and he turned to face the newcomer, who could not feel his heartbeat. Please, Susana touched the gringo's arm. Let go, you cheap whore, you promised me something, and if this guy's the problem then I'm getting him out of the way. No, you won't, that guy is my father. Holy Mary, Mother of God. Jason took aim again, but Arnold was focused on the detective and he had his dukes up.

Get into the bedroom, Doña Mary ordered the children and Susana. Wait a minute, you're wrong, I didn't promise you a thing or anyone else for that matter. But you're going out with this jerk, I've seen you. Now you know, he's my son's father and of course we have things we have to talk about. Of course, taking him to bed all week or maybe it's been longer. Hey, hey, fucking gringo, if the snit you're in is about me, leave the lady alone. Jason lowered his gun, suddenly he felt protected, and a pleasant sense of relief washed over his face. Lefty and the gringo eyed each other as if they were the first men to invade the moon and were battling for the hand of the king's daughter.

Arnold went at him, driven by a boundless rage born of race, social position, being in enemy territory and more. Lefty saw him coming, tried to dodge, but took a powerful right to the right shoulder that rocked him back. Shit. Doña Mary and Susana shrieked. Jason pulled them aside and put them in the bedroom with the children, who were peeking out excitedly; he told Gustavo to guard the door. Mendieta went at his rival's torso and kneed him in the crotch, but the man seemed unaffected; on the contrary, he landed a mighty blow on the detective's cheek, which made him

115

topple back. Jason, who had his revolver in his belt, caught him. But Mendieta had a temper, a brother who had been a guerrilla and a son to lose. I'm a badge, and in this country to be a badge you've got to be suicidal and nobody's role model, so you're going to suck my dick, asshole. With one swat a sweating Schwarzenegger knocked over the Christmas tree strung with coloured balls, while Mendieta broke a chair over his back, which made him smile.

Jason understood that Lefty had little chance of winning and got ready to rescue him: a bullet in the leg would put a dent in Arnold's bravery. But for Lefty the best offence was a good defence, he took advantage of his opponent's momentum to haul him crashing into a column and knee him in the belly. The gringo hit the floor with his hands, but got up as if nothing had happened. Lefty backed away. Is Robocop real? He opened the door and before stepping out he made a sign to the gringo to follow. The children, all a-twitter, lined up at the window.

Between the house and the low metal fence was a small garden, four by ten metres, that Doña Mary cared for like the daughter she always wanted: roses, gerberas, lilies, peace lilies, spearmint, a bougain-villea in one corner and in this season many poinsettias. The boxers traded punches near the roses. Jason watched from the doorway; the cousin who wanted to kill himself came out with a baseball bat signed by Adrián González, which Jason had brought him as a present. Mendieta, as best he could, got under the guard of Schwarzenegger, who blocked him and punched wildly, though he was beginning to show fatigue. Two minutes later, the fence was lined with neighbours. Men, women, children and dogs. A fist fight is something no-one in Culiacán wants to miss. They watched Arnold, who was a heavyweight, wallop Lefty, who was a born welterweight. A moment later they were shouting: Come on, Lefty, that faggot's going to fall, that's the way. Hit him down low, but fool him, fake him out. Lefty, don't stand still. Fuck that bag of steroids, my man Lefty, you can do it. In the liver, Lefty, hit him in the liver. Meanwhile, the detective danced and stung; something was happening to make him see Arnold's tremendous blows coming, evade them in time and hammer his own punches down low, where bit by bit it was feeling softer.

What was also happening was that the shouts were encouraging him and at the same time whittling away at the blondie, who knew this could not end well. Suddenly, without a word, he raised his hands, turned his back, pushed his way through the crowd and got into his pickup and raced off. The bros gave a light round of applause: That's my man Lefty, what fuckers. We'll be seeing you, Lefty. Well done, let those cocksuckers know who they're messing with. And they wandered back home to watch television. Mendieta looked at the shambles of the garden and turned toward a smiling Jason. I'm going home, clean all this up, would you? No, I'll go with you; Gustavo, tell Mama I'll be right back; let's go in the car, you're pretty beat up. In fact he was bleeding from the nose and mouth, his cheek was swollen, his ribs hurt, his clothes were torn and his boots were full of mud. Susana rushed out and climbed into the back seat, then started rubbing Lefty's shoulders, eliciting a yelp when she touched the right one. We'd better go to a clinic so they can check you out. It's not that bad. Are you sure?

Who was this woman he had fought for? He closed his eyes. What did it mean?

"Why it should be I have no clue, since I'm the kind who never forgets, but yet I must admit it's true, I forgot that I forgot you." Sincerely, El Cigala.

Twenty-Two

Dusk. Overcast again. Devil Urquídez and Drysnot inserted new magazines into their A.K.-47s at the same time. Click. Chopper Tarriba looked at them and caressed his bazooka. They were in Humaya Gardens guarding La Jefa, who had brought a bouquet of roses and a large framed photograph of a smiling Mariana. The mausoleums were small palaces with brilliantly coloured cupolas. Some featured Christmas decorations with potted poinsettias in the aisles. Others seemed abandoned. Cool breeze. Devil lit a cigarette. Drysnot was sweating. Ever since the events in Mazatlán impatience was the rule for him, he wanted to die, but with dignity, how could that asshole of a phantom have escaped him? when? he only got distracted for one second when a blonde gringa took off her wet T-shirt: What great tits, God, what itsy-bitsy underwear.

Inside the pink-tiled tomb, Samantha Valdés was praying before the photograph she had just hung. She crossed herself. Dearest, whoever it was will pay a high price, I promise you that, even if it brings the world to an end. The mausoleum smelled of roses and other flowers not yet wilted. Candles burning. Who was it? When you have so many enemies, you don't know where to start. It took a lot of balls to do this to me. You saw him, send me a sign so we can wring his neck sooner; I never knew of anyone who hated you enough to do this. It takes smarts to get around Max's guards; so he or they must have planned it really well. Suppose they were Max's enemies? Why fool myself: his enemies are my enemies, and yours too, just as mine are yours. She straightened a flower. I could exterminate the entire family of that traitor Eloy Quintana, but was it really them? My mother wants me to stop, what do you think? Eloy's wife is your comadre and I hear she's really upset. Honey, you have to give me a hand, who shot you? Oh, at home I've got that Sor Juana book you were so excited about, I promise I'll read it as soon as I can.

A pickup with tinted windows approached. Devil, Drysnot and the rest on alert. Guns at the ready. Hang on, Devil murmured, pointing his A.K., let them get a little closer; Chopper had them in his sights. The pickup rolled another ten metres and stopped; it sat unmoving for half a minute, then quickly reversed. Several bullet-holes were evident in one of the doors. The gunslingers relaxed and lit new cigarettes. Fear doesn't travel by burro, my man Devil. Neither does bravery, my man Drysnot; look smart because La Jefa just came out. They spied Samantha, who was immediately surrounded by men in dark caps. She went off in her car, and they followed.

Happy: they felt needed and chose not to remember.

Twenty-Three

They met up at Café Marimba on Niños Héroes Parkway for a carrot juice. I'm glad you got what you were after, fucking Faggot, they were at an outside table. Thanks to you. To me? don't fuck with me, I don't come anywhere near getting along with those bros: as far as I'm concerned the Valdés are the worst to ever come out of these parts. That's why my thank you is a big one. They drank: Estrada half the glass, Ugarte a sip. They're a bunch of bastards, they were in on me getting pinched and all that suffering I went through. Norah Jones' live version of "Don't Know Why" on the sound system. But you didn't rat on them. They only asked me about the old man at the beginning, later on when I wanted to talk about him or mentioned him as responsible, the uniforms played deaf, they wanted to know about everyone except that scum. Not only are they obviously powerful, they seem to know how to stay on top. Don't doubt it, fucking Faggot, they've got half the world paid off. Hey, for a business to run well that's what it takes, no? If you say so, aren't you the expert? The best part was that the weather was fucking great. Listen, now that we're into it, there's a big fat rumour making the rounds that the meeting got out of hand, did you see anything? What do you mean? Word is there was shooting, bodies and broken windows. Really? not while I was around, as soon as it was over I was out of there, and the rest of them did the same. People say there was a gunfight and several bros got whacked. Well, like I say, not while I was there, you say people got killed? You know I don't know shit, that's what the guys are saying. And even if you knew you wouldn't let it slip, you're a time capsule, I.B.M. Not about that stuff, you know anything that has to do with the Valdés family means shit to me; and now that you're retired what's next? are you going to start up that bordello for under-twenties you talked about, to teach the youth how to enjoy themselves in bed instead of being fucking wankers? Even better: I'm going to die. Well, of course, what did you think, asshole, you were going to stick around for fucking ever? you aren't such fucking hot shit. I've got colon cancer, he didn't want to say prostate. A sudden breeze. Are you serious or are you just being a fucking jerk? Nope, serious. They both looked down to the river's edge, where willows cast their shadows. That's why you're so pasty? My friend, I've only got a couple of months left, and I'm going to spend it with my family. You always were a henpecked husband. It's my best option. Did you get a second opinion? A scrapbook full of them and they all say the same thing, plus that an operation would be fatal. Fucking Faggot, the fact is you're always doing wild shit and you talk about it like it was nothing. This is our goodbye, I.B.M. Another long look at the river, grey under the cloudy sky. That cancer, is it common for people our age? They never told me, do you remember Miranda, that guy in high school who was always so spiffed up? Of course, fucking Oriental, more fat-faced than his fucking mother. One day I ran into him in Phoenix at one of those high-tech oncology clinics, he had something on his skin. So it turns out I'm the healthy one. You've already got dementia, buddy, and your ups and downs are nothing to spit at, or have you forgotten how much you scream at night? They drank. Listen, don't give St Peter too much shit. I won't, you'll see when you turn up. And don't be pulling my feet after you, asshole. They way they stink, the thought won't cross my mind. And here I was thinking colon had to do with Columbus and all the little Christophers that came after. They smiled.

Dense gunfire could be heard coming from the Botanical Gardens; both of them shook their heads as if to say there was no fixing it. I'm going to be better off up there. No fucking way am I tempted, Faggot, not until my number comes up. What's come up is your turn to pay. Even halfdead you're still a sponger. Estrada fell silent, suddenly his friend's face looked different. Bones and dark cavities without much to sweeten them. He closed his eyes and the clarity blinded him.

Twenty-Four

On Monday Mendieta woke up a wreck. Not only did everything still hurt but he felt rattled by Susana's invasion of his space, she had stayed late to watch over him. A few glasses of whisky before bed had worked to wake him up early enough, but they did not ease the pain; as soon as he considered it prudent he gave Zelda Toledo a call. Don't forget to bring Gori in this afternoon, I didn't get to it yesterday; he needs his self-esteem back and we have to lend him a hand. Jason turned up early, gave him the number from the black pickup's plates and the name of the hotel where Arnold Schwarzenegger was staying. Though the guy had broken the law, Lefty decided to do nothing unless he turned up to bother Susana again; if the asshole keeps at it I'll toss him in the slammer. Then his mind drifted back to the young sexy girl he once took to Sandy's restaurant on Obregón long ago: Two hamburgers with jalapeños, fries, two Cokes and two malteds, one vanilla and one chocolate. Mine with double tomato, double cheese and lime.

He sized himself up in the mirror: a cut over one eye, which was half shut, mouth swollen, cheek purple and inflamed; his body scratched and bruised in several places; his legs aching. Fucking gringo, I guess he wanted to kill me, and all for Susana, who'd have ever guessed I'd live through this little episode for her? A girl who hated having a boyfriend because she wanted to go out with every-one, who surprised him by asking him out for a stroll. I'll only go if you have supper with me afterwards. Ha, and who told you anyone puts conditions on me? That's one I'll answer at supper. She was lovely, a perfect body; one of those women you can't ignore because there was also her aggressive way of kissing, of hugging you tight, of making love. Two hamburgers. What a dream. Our fling had barely begun when she vanished; I missed her for a couple of weeks; a badge's work is so crazy you can't afford such luxuries. In the Col Pop no-one spoke of her again because Rafaella turned up, a redhead with pink nipples who people said loved rough sex. I never got involved. At the last minute, Susana changed her mind: Listen, could you make that a steak with potatoes and a michelada? Not that I remember, but for sure the waiter was not pleased.

Cavalry charge. Mendieta. Boss, Gori isn't any better, in fact he hasn't even come into Headquarters and the people from Narcotics have two kids who don't want to spill the beans. Let me call him. In the kitchen Trudis was singing "Oye Cómo Va", her voice loud, confident. He dialled. Good morning, señora, please put Gori on the line. He's in the shower. Pull him out, tell him it's Detective Mendieta. Lefty? What, is there another? It's just that he's really depressed. Other people get depressed, get him on the telephone right now. Pause. My man Lefty, I'll be in soon. Don't give me that soon shit, Gori, did you turn queer or what? What's that about, my man Lefty, why are you saying that? Now it turns out you're afraid of a pathetic loser. It's not fear, I know what fear is and it's not fear, what's going on is I want to resign. Don't mess with me, fucking Gori, especially now; the day before yesterday I ran into the guy, I called him on his behaviour and he beat me to a pulp, you won't believe the way he left me, he swore you're a fucking faggot from the slums and said you sucked his dick, he even threatened to go find your wife so she would have the chance to do it with at least one man in her life, not the despicable wretch she lives with. The fucking sonofabitch said that? Well, I told him we were going to get him this afternoon and he laughed and just repeated that you're a loser and since you're going to resign he'd take your place. That face-like-my-ass, he's going to be royally fucked. My man Gori, get yourself to the office right now and beat the shit out of two kids who raped a girl your daughter's age, they're going to tell you they're hired guns, but they're rapists, fuck them over and I'll see you there.

He showered very gingerly. Jason arrived in time for a breakfast of fish machaca. He texted, then put away his cell. If only Lefty would shave you two would look like twins, Trudis sang out while serving them, and they both smiled. Suppose I let my beard grow, Trudis? Absolutely not, you look good as you are; you should have brought your mother. She's still sleeping, thank you; Edgar, if you want I could be your driver, your left eye is practically swollen shut. Thanks, Zelda Toledo will do that. So, what do you think of this nectar of the gods? Delicious; hey, did you try the Nescafé? You know Trudis won't give me anything else, you're going to have to send me a jar every so often, what about your present? A big smile: You already gave it to me, it's what you did yesterday, you got that gringo off our backs. Mendieta's eyes met Jason's and he detected the shine of a young man who felt safe, almost pampered. He had a sudden urge which he refused to analyse, he got to his feet and in the light of Trudis's broad smile he said: Give me a hug, kid. Jason jumped up and they melted into each other's arms. Uggh, careful. Lefty felt his eyes well up, but he blocked the sob; the one who could not was Trudis, who had tears running down her cheeks; she imagined the fathers of her own children treating them like that and making them happy. Ring. Trudis went to the telephone, taking her time. Ring. Hello, just a moment please, she turned toward the pair, who at that moment were unfastening their embrace: It's Captain Pineda.

How's it going, Mendieta? Never better, but what can you do, and you? In the shit, the bros won't stop massacring each other just because it's Christmas, this is a genuine social movement. That must be a present from Santa Claus. A present from Santa Claus is what I have for you: a few days ago we found a body in a cornfield near Navolato, the man had been reported missing, his family identified him and we even handed over the body. So? He was a dentist, Ortega says they used the same weapons to take down another dentist you know about. O.K., death to the fucking dentists. I gave the info to Ortega in case it's of any use to you. Thanks and have a merry Christmas. You too, Lefty what-a-sight.

He dialled Zelda. Agent Toledo, Pineda tells me another dentist was murdered, same weapons as Manzo; find Ortega, he's got the details on the dead guy, have you seen Montaño? He has no business here. Don't get touchy, call his cell and ask him to call me. Only because it's you.

He did not want to return to the table, he was feeling nauseous and eating only made it worse. Should I take you to the doctor?

Jason could see how pale he was. Trudis too: Lie down, Lefty, you look really sick. Let's wait a while, the T-shirt was bothering him and when he took it off Trudis was shocked. Yikes, they nearly killed you, let me put some yerba manza and arnica on you, I'll go ask the lady across the street for a few leaves. Wait, you can do that later. You know what, Lefty? this is bad, I don't like it, you'd better go to the doctor, let young Jason take you. I'll take him. Mendieta's cell rang out. Yes? It was Montaño. Where are you? At my little lair, Lefty, like I told you, you wouldn't believe how useful it turned out to be. Is she really lovely? She's going to try for Miss Sinaloa, that should say it all. Watch out a narco doesn't snatch her. Well, it's not like I want to marry her. I need you to come, day before yesterday I got jumped and my stomach's all purple. Are you serious? My head spins and I have trouble breathing. Where are you? At home in the Col Pop. Don't move, I'll be right there. Bring the miss. None of that, she's going to stay here and study for the contest, she still thinks global warming is the best thing that's happened in years.

Half an hour later Montaño nearly confused Jason with Lefty. Wow, Lefty, this boy is yours, eh, he couldn't look any more like you. Only good things get repeated, right, Jason? Absolutely. Montaño checked his abdomen, his cheek, his eye, took his blood pressure. What was this all about, Mendieta, did they catch you sleeping? More or less. He poked him. Ugh. They beat you everywhere; I'm going to give you an injection, but you should stay in bed for a few hours. How many? Six should be enough. That's too many. Jason can take your place, I mean, he'd probably like the

128

police. I'm going to be a policeman, doctor. Well, that's that, take your father's place for the next six hours. Stop it, Montaño, don't put ideas in his head, he's barely eighteen. I'm not saying he should shoot anyone or anything, just sit in your office so they see you're on the job. We'll think about it, what about you? shouldn't you turn up to oversee your interns once in a while? Every day; remember, they're all young women eager to learn and, well, it seems I'm a good teacher; listen, if anything happens give me a call, I'll be right there. Thank you, and watch out, there's a hay fever going around. Right, try to sleep, it'll take effect more quickly. Doctor, can I put on some yerba manza and arnica? Of course you can, and keep an eye on him, don't let him slip out the door.

Jason accompanied him to the bedroom and helped Trudis put on the plasters.

At seven that evening, less sore, dark glasses in place and swelling on the way down, he met up with Gori at Headquarters. All set? As set as the table for a twelve-course meal, my man Lefty; wait, you don't look good, that faggot beat the shit out of you. It's nothing compared to what we're going to do to him, right? Then Zelda brought them up to date on the murder of Dr Antonio Estolano, a prestigious orthodontist from Navolato: according to the forensic doctor he was killed the day after Manzo by a bullet from a Herstal; his assistant said she left him alone with the last patient since it was an easy job, just pulling a shard of glass from his gums. What? You heard right, it was a man who makes his living in bars chewing beer bottles and mugs for tips. Did you locate him? A narco took him out to his farm to put on a show, but tomorrow at six he'll be at La Flor de Capomo where he usually works; his name is José Rodelo and they call him the Glasseater. O.K., we'll go see him tomorrow, now we have to find Blake Hernández. Is it true he beat you up too? Isn't it obvious? he took off his glasses. My God, let me go with you. No way, I want you to buy presents for yourself, Angelita, Gori, Ortega, Montaño and Robles. Nothing for the commander? Alright, buy him a spoon or something for his kitchen. Chief, don't forget about your son or his mother. You can help me with that later on. Can I take Angelita along? Like when you two go to the bathroom? Close enough, we'll go to the Forum. O.K., don't turn off your cell; he pulled an envelope with money from his desk and gave it to her. And by the way, how's Jason? Handsome as could be, just like his father; let's go, Gori. If you're going to cook it tonight, you've got to start soaking it now, my man Lefty; you have a son? So it seems. Congratulations, was he just born? He's eighteen, my man Gori. No kidding, and I thought you'd never married. Well, now you know.

Blake Hernández had his auto-parts business on Heroico Colegio Militar Highway, in the south of the city. They went out on Zapata, took Pascual Orozco and as soon as they turned the corner were surrounded by two Hummers and two pickups, all of them black. What a fucking mess. Gori got nervous: Lefty, what's this all about? Easy, my man Gori, I hope you've made out your will. I'm fucked. All five vehicles came to a standstill. Did we bring anything to defend ourselves? Well, I don't think my Walther will get us out of this one. I don't even have that. Men climbed out of three of the black vehicles, rifles in hand; one of them was Max Garcés.

Twenty-Five

Ugarte's cell phone rang. He was walking listlessly down a hallway at Benito Juárez Airport in Mexico City, dragging a small suitcase and carrying a bag of dried shrimp he had bought at Best Mar. He decided to take the call. How are you this morning, General? Sleepless, what about you? Doing my thing, headed for the market right now. Are you still in Culiacán? About to take a taxi to my hideaway. To your private hell. Exactly. Listen, I heard a rumour they killed the señora's girlfriend the night of the meeting, what do you know about that? What? That's right, can you corroborate the story? While we were with her the señora didn't seem upset at all, we didn't hear anything nor did anyone mention it, and then we all left immediately like we were supposed to. Could you look into it? people are telling me that's what's behind the wave of violence washing across the country. Uh-oh, that is serious, the cure turned out to be worse than the disease. If it's true, it means that group we haven't managed to identify and which must be very powerful is on the rise. Anyone in particular? No idea. What about the Secretary? We're watching him, for the moment just keep your eyes peeled, you may have to intervene. I'm sorry, General, but you can't count on me for that, right now I'm an elephant on the way to his graveyard; what I will do is make a call. I understand, and the last thing I want to do is trouble you, but the situation is critical. That group you mentioned won't be my job. Are you really in such a bad way? General, I'm not in a bad, way I'm seriously ill. O.K. then, I'll expect your call.

Fucking Faggot, I was just thinking of you. I think I'm going to take your advice, I.B.M., I won't celebrate my birthday until January. That's quite the fucking month, it's got the long climb out of the Christmas hole, all sorts of sales and it's fucking cold; when I was crossing off the days it was the toughest month, more suicides and killings than any other time of year. In La Jolla it wasn't pretty either, always cloudy, empty streets, Chinese food, that was when I visited you twice a week and you couldn't stop talking about what you would do when you got out; if I wanted you to stop flapping your gums all I had to do was ask you about somebody. Keeping my trap shut sent me to purgatory, but that's all in the past; listen, what fart's got you worried, because you don't call just to say hello. It's good we know all about each other, isn't it? Good and bad, what the fuck's up? the suspense is killing me. Is it true they killed Mariana Kelly?

Silence of an orchestra, eyes on the conductor.

Supposedly it happened while we were in the meeting, is that what you meant when you said there was a gunfight? There's something to that. What do you mean there's something to that? tell me if it happened or it didn't. Hey, hey, what's this about, fucking Faggot, are you going to squeeze my balls until I tell you? you can suck my dick. Sorry, don't get offended, it's because I'm feeling sick, I'll call you later, I've got to run to the bathroom.

He hung up, he was at a pay phone; then he dialled the General.

Twenty-Six

A worried Gori drove the Toyota back to S.M.P. Headquarters. Zelda and Angelita were leaving for the Forum as he came in the door. What happened? He filled them in. It was like they'd been tailing him, my girl Zelda, the guy that looked to be in charge said hello, called him by his name and asked him to go with them. But how did the boss react, did they drag him off or what? No, he just told me to wait for him here. I don't like this, not one bit, they might have put the snatch on him to kill him, that's the narcos' style and you know the boss can't stand them. He seemed pretty calm to me. Zelda dialled his cell, after three rings she heard: I'm O.K., I'll see you in a little while. The junior detective grew thoughtful. If you like we can leave the presents for tomorrow. No, Angelita, let's do it now; Gori, we're going to the Forum, do you want to come with us? Only if you'll do me a favour, Zelda my girl. Tell me. First take me to the buddy who beat me up, I can't wait any longer for another shot at him, may it turn out however God wishes. Zelda fixed her gaze on the torturer, then on Angelita. Do you want to stay here? Why can't I go along? you know I've never seen Hortigosa in action. Gori, you'll have two fans in the front row; we'll go from there to get the presents, this time of year they're open late. Smiling, they sang: "Pa rum pum pum, hit the bum bum, give the dum-dum a glass of rum rum rum."

Through the window beside the entrance to Blake's Auto Parts, they could see him in his office speaking on the telephone. Zelda went in first. A few Christmas lights, customers, ranchera music. Señorita, what are you doing here? You still haven't told me what you were up to the night Dr Humberto Manzo Solís was killed. And I'm not going to tell you, didn't I make that clear? Clear as could be, your brother sent us pictures of what we didn't do to you. But you would have if I'd let you, don't deny it. The detective smiled: Those are things we would never do even if you still refused to cooperate. Lips pressed, jaw set, Gori approached. It was an open-plan office and they were in full view of the staff and customers, who at that time of day numbered about half a dozen. You brought your orangutan? He wanted to come along, I guess he likes you. Gori went right up to his executioner, he was eager to overcome his fear and knew he had to face it head on. Blake stood up. I don't want any fighting in my shop. Who's talking about fighting? sputtered Zelda. Behind them, Angelita wrung her hands. If we're going to tussle, I'd rather we step outside, the engineer said firmly. Gori feinted with his left, but his opponent was not fooled and answered with a right to the stomach that left him green around the gills. Ugh. The staff and customers turned toward them. Two employees picked up metal bars to help their boss, but Zelda held them back. Take it easy, bros, this is a private matter and that's how it has to be settled, go back where you were. Blake nodded.

He waited for Gori to recover and come at him muttering: How could you dare bring my family into this, asshole. He even allowed Gori to land a couple of blows on his face, but then he hit him again down low and on the chin so hard the man teetered.

Zelda stepped between them. Señor Blake, where were you the night Dr Manzo was killed? The engineer was sweaty and triumphant, sparks flying from his eyes: I'm not going to tell you, what, are you retarded? Gori flipped the desk over, shattered two lamps, and smashed the telephone on the floor. That's for what you did to the boss, asshole, my business we'll take up another time. The two employees again tried to intervene, but Zelda threatened to give them Christmas presents they might not have deserved. The customers, astonished, excited and very attentive, did not miss a thing; the staff were wondering: Who is this broad who thinks she's so tough? Everyone was mystified.

Let's leave it at that, Blake murmured. This man can't beat me and I'm not going to say where I was that night, and I didn't kill that idiot Manzo; as you might have noticed, I wouldn't have needed a gun, a punch in the right spot would have done the trick. You were not at home that night, Señor Blake, Zelda maintained her intimate tone, Angelita took Gori's arm and pulled him stumbling from the room, several customers departed after making their purchases, the traffic outside was intense. That's true, but I did not go out at eight o'clock at night to kill that guy. How do you know when it happened? Because Lizzie told me. They glared at each other. I'm not satisfied with your response, Señor Blake, we'll be seeing you again. Bring a warrant instead of the orangutan and maybe I'll tell you something, but it won't be what you expect to hear. Then you're the retard.

Zelda stalked out, seriously annoyed. Gori was waiting in the back seat, crushed, in pain. Hey, enough of that face, the guy respects you, he told me he thinks you're the best and he doesn't want any hard feelings; he was national kickboxing champion and he just retired undefeated, he asks you to forgive him and let it die there. Gori brightened a bit: He can go fuck himself, the pansy, forgive him is the last thing I would do, the bastard not only beat me twice, he beat up Lefty too, just wait until I get him on my turf. He's an animal, and the boss is such a nice guy. Gori, give me two days and I'll have him for you at Headquarters. Seven years' bad luck if you don't, Zelda my girl. The women smiled. Let's go to the Forum; Gori, start thinking about what present you want from Chief Mendieta. A bottle of tequila and a case of beer. Hey, you can't get drunk, suppose you run into Blake? Don't worry, Zelda, to get smashed I need three times as much.

Then he fell silent, his expression grim. How did I end up in all this? First I was training to be a wrestler, I didn't have the dough to buy the trunks, never mind a mask. That was when I met Lefty, we were just kids, and it didn't take much to convince me to go into police work. In the beginning if the bad guys didn't want to confess I broke their bones, then I learned where to hit and how hard. Everything was going great until I met up with this faggot, how many has he beaten up anyway? He did a number on Lefty too; poor boss, his chest is all bandaged, his face all puffy and one eye's swollen shut. I don't think I can beat that bro, he's really quick and he knows how to punch and where; that is, unless I put a bullet in him.

Zelda turned on the stereo: Air Supply's "Making Love Out of Nothing at All". She saw Angelita closing her eyes; she pulled out on to the highway feeling she loved Rodo more every day. Fucking Rodo.

Twenty-Seven

They met in the bungalow in the garden at the mansion in Colinas de San Miguel, her father's favourite spot for receiving visitors. Poinsettias and a few Christmas decorations in view. Dim lighting. César ran in to say goodbye: he was going to Altata with Minerva and three bodyguards. Don't annoy your grandmother, eh? behave yourself. Mama, I love you so much, he kissed her and hurried out. Nine years old. He smelled of Fahrenheit for Men. Luigi was on the lawn, alert, eyes trained on the driveway gate: that was where his mistress would arrive, if she did. Without a word a young man served two whiskies on the rocks and left the bottle on the table. You look kind of beat-up, Lefty, what happened? Me, I slipped on a grape skin. Samantha Valdés shook her head as if to say, You'll never learn. Well, first things first, she said; the detective waited uncomfortably, his mind a blank. Congratulations on Jason, we know he's a good boy, no doubt he'll go far. You know about him? He's popular, a good student, a champion in the mile with a good shot at making the Olympics. What does this woman have in mind? They drank. The mother is lovely, isn't she? and has she ever managed to keep her looks. She had a portrait painted that does the aging for her, do you really know about all that? This city is small and, like my mother says, we're all neighbours. Several hired guns were posted at strategic spots around the discreetly lit garden; the dog sat unmoving. Second of all, and she rushed the words, her

137

habitually severe expression softening, a wistful look in her eyes: They killed Mariana. The detective felt shocked, he guessed he must have widened his eyes because his bruise hurt. They killed her, Lefty Mendieta, in Mazatlán, Saturday before last; we were there, I left her alone in her room for a short while and when I went back she had a bullet-hole in her forehead. The detective filled his host's glass and she tossed it back, he filled it again, as well as his own. That woman was a sweetheart, Lefty, she wanted to do good, she wanted to build a hospital for children with cancer and clinics in poor neighbourhoods. Silence for thinking about nothing. You lose a man and you get over it, you listen to sappy songs and that's that, but when you lose a woman you lose part of yourself, a really big part, do you understand what I'm saying? Silence. Don't think it's a rib or a liver, like they say, it's a slice of your heart or your soul, I don't know. Were you at a hotel? The Estrella Reluciente, we were planning to spend a couple of days there, but as you can see God makes mistakes too; she drank; I want you to find the murderer and bring him to me. Samantha, I respect your grief and I agree what a good person Mariana was, but I'm not a private investigator, I'm a badge, and as you once told me one of the stupidest. You don't think I know what you are or remember how hard I was on you? she drank again; I invited you once before to come closer to us and you said you'd think about it. Silence. I'm asking you as a personal favour, she stood up, peered out the window at the garden; she had a high regard for you, she told me so without any prompting, and I feel really awful, she turned to face the detective; there's a huge hole at my side, Lefty Mendieta, and I don't know how to fill it, I feel like shit, more dead than alive, worse than that poor animal you see over there. Lefty brought his glass to his lips, he did not want to get involved, but he felt touched. Samantha's eyes, although dry, were shiny. Did you go for the weekend? More or less. The woman returned to her seat. I know you aren't ambitious, that you aren't very interested in money, however, I want you to know that you can ask for whatever you like, I'll pay anything to get that bastard in my clutches, or that bitch, Samantha added firmly. Did you go to the police? No, and I stopped the hotel people from doing it. Is it you ordering these killings? Power feeds on blood, Lefty Mendieta, you understand, right? No, I don't, and neither do I want you to explain. Silence. It's fucking crushing me and I know my methods aren't going to get me anywhere; so I need you, Mariana needs you, you bastard. Lefty closed his eyes and hurried his drink. How did you know about Jason? The girl he went to Altata with is the daughter of one of my men, at some point he mentioned you, she told her father and Chino told me. Mendieta looked at his hands. Have they rented out the room where Mariana died? Not yet, Max will give you the details. Get me a white van without tinted windows and money to take the technical team to Mazatlán. You've got it. One other thing: suspend the butchery. She looked at him: Do you really think we can do that? No, but it would help me understand the woman you're missing, I always had the impression she was a pacifist. You're an asshole. Thank you for the kind words about Jason, isn't it risky to let your son go to Altata? You know it is, but I don't want to deprive him of certain things; I hope I don't come to regret it. And you hope darkness lends a hand. Precisely.

How many days were you at the hotel? A few hours only, we went to a private meeting to reach agreement on staying out of the war, but as you can see they made me lose all interest in negotiating. I get that, do you suspect anyone? No-one in particular, it couldn't be just anyone; I've thought and thought and come up with nothing; I know that hurting people is inevitable, lots of times you don't even notice. What can you tell me about Eloy's group? You're starting off on the right foot, what I can't understand is how they managed to get to her. Figuring that out will be our job. They shook hands. Do you think you'll have something by Christmas? To be Santa Claus, all I need is the beard. And the belly, by the way I hope you enjoy your present, she signalled and Garcés stepped in. What are you talking about? She raised her hands to say it was nothing. Give him whatever he needs, and you, Lefty Mendieta, thank you for accepting. Garcés asked the detective to follow him.

The small office used by Ulises, the accountant. A cold, dark, belligerent stare: I'm listening. Mendieta repeated his requirements. Garcés handed him a wad of five-hundred-peso bills and another of fifty-dollar bills. If that doesn't cover it, send one of the boys for more. What boys? The two I'm giving you for whatever you might need, one of them is a friend of yours. Devil Urquídez? That's the one. Have him bring his wife along, I hope you don't mind if I give them a few days for their honeymoon. Fine with me, just don't be reckless; the other is Chopper Tarriba, he's a good friend of Devil's and you can trust him. Let them both know I'm the one giving the orders. Garcés smiled an ironic smile. By the way, we're still paying for Mariana's room and the one the señora used, that's helpful, right? Well, I hope I'm not going to find your fingerprints anywhere compromising, do you know what weapon they used? We didn't find any shell or casing, I hope you'll have better luck. La Jefa mentioned a private meeting, I should know who was there. I'm not authorised to give you that information. Seriously? Ask her yourself, though I don't think it will be much use, they were all very loyal people. The cemeteries are filled with loyal people; listen, she talked about a present, do you know anything about it? Ah, that's about the gringo who beat you up. What about him? We put him down, and don't worry about the body. Lefty touched his tender chest to keep from feeling guilty. What sort of van do you need? One that will hold five or six people comfortably and carry a couple of suitcases of equipment. In two hours we'll drop it off at your house. If I'm not there, leave the key on the floor by the door; tell the boys we'll be leaving tomorrow at seven, if they can't make that, they can meet us at the hotel.

The power of the green bills had Ortega and two of his technicians inspecting every inch of the hotel room the following day. The detective, eyes wide open, went in and out of the room by the hallway door and the one that connected it to Samantha's room. He paused in the middle of the small living area where the crime took place, let his gaze wander, went over to the window, inspected the mechanism for opening it; next door he did the same, they were identical. There were no telling odours. Zelda Toledo came in from interrogating the staff and scrutinised everything. They agreed that the window, which closed very securely, was a point to consider. Mendieta wrote that down in his notebook, and Zelda took photographs. Then they went into the garden, which extended to the golf course. They contemplated the facade of the building that contained the window in question: smooth surface, two floors above it and one below. The gunslinger keeping watch did not notice anything unusual or see anyone, Garcés had told him that, even so they would speak with him when they got back to Culiacán. Señor Mendieta, I'm here for whatever you might need, Chopper introduced himself, he was short, about twenty years old, eyes probing the depths. For now, just stay alert, did Devil carry out my orders? Like lightning. Good, keep watch, stand under that rubber tree, and if you see the murderer return to the scene of the crime, you will have achieved something unheard-of these days. The young man smiled and moved off. Zelda, do we have a list of the guests? We do: fifty-three rooms occupied by gringos and Canadians, plus twenty-two reserved on the same date by a Señor P.C., the only ones still here are a pair of elderly gringos. That P.C. and his people, how many nights did they stay? Not even one, the day of the murder they arrived after three in the afternoon and before ten that night they were gone; most of them stayed about five hours, at least that's what the report says. Interesting, did he leave an address, telephone, email, anything to locate him? Nothing, all those things were left blank and the manager says he doesn't know why, that's how they gave it to him in reservations; the reservations people can't say why those details were omitted. Anything but an impossible case, the detective reflected. How does Señor Pacific Cartel strike you? How brazen can you get?

Are the gringos in their room? We'll have to see. Zelda looked at the list, went down six doors and knocked. A thin man about seventy-five years old answered. *Buenos días.* No Spanish. Zelda made signs for him to wait a moment. Boss, they don't speak Spanish. What about Aramaic? They're learning it now, what should we do? Mendieta thought a minute and dialled his house. Trudis, find Jason and ask him to call me. He's here, Lefty, he came over for breakfast, where are you? In Mazatlán, put him on. Since your car is here I got frightened, is your chest still hurting? No, I'm fine, thank you. What's up? Jason on the line. I'm in Mazatlán on a case, I've got two elderly white gringos who don't speak Spanish, I want you to ask them these questions, he listed them. Got it, put them on.

A few moments later Jason told him she was deaf, that night they were settling in for the evening, they never heard any shots, they had no idea there was a body a few steps from their room, and the señora was watching a Frank Sinatra movie. They agreed to meet up that night.

O.K., let's take a look at the roof. Hallway, elevator, a flight of stairs. It looked as though it had recently been waterproofed, and they found the remains of some takeout food. They paused by the cornice more or less above the window to Mariana's room. Zelda, you'd better call Ortega, find the head of maintenance and ask him when they put on the waterproofing.

What is it I'm not seeing or feeling or smelling? He recalled a movie where the thief rappelled down into a museum on a very thin wire. Something like Tom Cruise in "Mission Impossible", but that guy was crazy; I guess the one who did this little job is not exactly what you would call sane. Every homicide has a backstory wrapped around an enigma, what could it be in this case?

Now what do you want, cocksucker, aren't you tired of fucking with me? The criminal might have rappelled down, I want you to see if there's any sign of it and if that tells us anything. Great, now we're going to catch Spider-Man? Ortega looked around, took some pictures of the surface and the cornice, which had a tiny groove on the edge that might have been made by a thin wire. It was hidden by the waterproofing, but Ortega was an old hand and he used his pocketknife to peel off the new black layer.

They waterproofed last Sunday, Zelda reported. So the footprints on the roof won't be his, said Ortega, who was carefully inspecting the groove and now with his pocketknife was uncovering a six-centimetre hole drilled through the concrete. Look at this. The detectives came over. He could have threaded a very fine wire with a block on the end through here, then stepped off and lowered himself down, Mendieta concluded. Well, your brain's working, isn't it? your son must have lit a fire under you. Lefty leaned over to look at the wall below the point where the perforation lay: it lined up with the window. Zelda took his picture. Looks just like you; we'll give you some elbow room, see what else you can find. Zelda, get the grounds staff and the gardeners together and ask if they found anything unusual; we're looking for rock-climbing equipment and maybe clothing. You think he wore camouflage? No, I'm just guessing that might lead us somewhere. He might have made his escape wearing whatever he had on, but did he go down to the ground? back up the wall? Maybe he took the elevator. What colour is the wall? Brick, Ortega said. Boss, the colour of the staff uniform is reddish too, with the name of the hotel in black.

They say real life takes place somewhere else.

Twenty-Eight

Cuernavaca. Ugarte was sleeping fitfully in a comfortable bedroom with a large window that gave on to a garden of hedges, bougain-villea and assorted flowering plants. Several potted poinsettias underscored the red. His pain and pallor were extreme. No way could he put off telling his family any longer: I'm sorry. His wife María took it stoically, somehow she already knew, sharing her life with this mysterious man had prepared her for a moment such as this, but not Francelia, his daughter. She thought the world of her father, believed he had rendered invaluable service to his country and did not deserve to die so young; he hadn't even cele-brated his sixtieth, he'd postponed it to December and now he was claiming there were too many parties that month, better to do it in January; January? he might not be around to tell the story, to tell her his story, as he had promised, and nothing could be worse for her, since she was dreaming of following in his footsteps.

It was the girl who interrupted him. Pa, General Alvarado is on the line. He put aside the little Bible resting on his chest and took the portable telephone she held out.

James Taylor softly singing "You've Got a Friend".

Three hours later he was facing the Secretary on the eighth floor of the Four Seasons in Mexico City, in the presidential suite. Man One, Man Two, Man Three stood at a prudent distance. Dark suits. On the wall, photographs of giraffes and elephants. The

Secretary was drinking vodka and had him served a glass of beer, which he would not even taste. What's the story with that meeting, Señor Ugarte, did they lose their minds? have you seen how the number of killings has gone through the roof? what really happened, did they decide to trash the whole country? because I didn't learn nearly enough from your reports and neither did the President; the following day six bodies were found hanging from a bridge in Mazatlán, right where they met, why did you hide the fact that they agreed to attack? There was no such agreement, Señor Secretary, I told you exactly what they spoke about and I did not perceive in any of them a desire to escalate the violence or the confrontation with your side. Well, the President is not pleased with your work. Or with yours, right? That is none of your business, tell me again the names of the people present. All the members of the Pacific Cartel were represented: you know the names better than I. You listen to me, Ugarte! you fucked up, you shat all over this operation, it was a failure, and you are to blame; I told the President as much, and your protector too. Ugarte stood up. Then we have nothing more to talk about, my duty was to tell you what was discussed, who attended and what it was I did; it is not my job to draw conclusions or decide on any plan of action; if the violence worsened you must know why, that's the reason you were appointed. You aren't going to tell me what my job is, you double-oh-shit. Nor are you going to humiliate me as if I were an imbecile and your little war was going just fine. Shut up and sit down. Man One and Man Two, brandishing automatic pistols in their right hands, seized him by the arms and pushed him into his chair. Who are you, Ugarte? that guy

Alvarado sold us on you saying you were in the Special Service, but we couldn't find your name anywhere in their records, is your name really Héctor Ugarte? The agent's eyes were ablaze: As you ought to understand, I will not answer your question, you should know who lives in this country, if you don't, I can't fathom how you think you can keep it under control; and by the way what make-up do you use? because some of it is showing. The men smiled but did not budge from their positions on either side of the pallid agent, whose lips were trembling and who began to feel nausea and a terrible weakness overpowering his rage. The Secretary tossed back his drink. Man Three refilled his glass immediately. Why have you switched to vodka now? The Secretary smiled: That night in Mazatlán something happened that you should have seen coming. I managed to get what you sent me for and I got you my report on time. Yes, and you fled immediately. The same as everyone else. Did you not know they killed the señora's girlfriend? He prudently took his time answering: Is that it? no, I did not know, and of course that has nothing to do with me, since it did not occur at the meeting. Well, that's what set off this wave of violence. How brilliant of you. I want to know if you observed anything unusual, or saw anyone who would dare to provoke Samantha Valdés like that. My job was to attend the meeting, listen, report to you and disappear right away; I did not pay attention to anything else, and of course there was no hint of that. The Secretary downed his glass, then gave his interlocutor a scornful look: I don't want to see you ever again in my life. Ugarte stood up, despite the pain, and walked out with difficulty; when he got out of the elevator he went to the bathroom and vomited; then, paler than ever, he let himself be led by a Yucatecan in a green guayabera, who took him to a car and drove him home to his house in the beautiful city of eternal spring.

To be what you are, that is the problem, he gave a Shakespearian sigh as they rode along Paseo de la Reforma, secure in the knowledge that his remaining days were dwindling and that for every action there is a reaction. He opened his eyes, and there it was again, more distinct than ever, the only one in no hurry. The avenue was all lit up, excessively so. Of course, December is a month of many parties.

Twenty-Nine

They gathered in one of the hotel's small meeting rooms. Nothing out of the ordinary: name, occupation, where they had been between seven and nine the night of the crime; that is, until they came to Chickenmite, a thin man with a small moustache who could make the most inhospitable sandpit bloom: I remember that day, I was working on the rose beds in the back, and the key lady asked me for two dozen roses, the showiest, because they were for the private room where the heavyweights were going to meet. A meeting of heavyweights, where? Mendieta exchanged a glance with Zelda. You people are from the police, you can't not know. When? Don't play games with me, bossman; anyhow, I took the flowers in about seven-thirty, I had a Coke and I went back to get my things because that was the end of my shift, though I still pruned a couple of rose bushes, because it's better to do that at night; then I heard a noise, something dropped into the dumpster near me, right up against the wall; I thought it came from the roof and I went over to take a look: it was a uniform all balled up. Same as yours? Same colour, but it seemed nicer; I looked up at the roof, but I didn't see anyone. Do you still have it? No, I looked at it and left it, who knows where it would be now, they pick up the trash every day. Alright, señores, which of you threw a uniform off the roof? What uniform, since we only get one. And we knock off at seven, this guy sticks around longer because he's into it, he even talks to the plants. They haven't given me a uniform in two years. Five or six of them spoke up at the same time. O.K., all of you back to work, only Chickenmite stays behind. Badge buddy, put an end to the violence, I've had it with all this killing. Sure, that's a promise, it'll be your Christmas present. You're too skinny to play Santa Claus, my badge-man, I think you're spouting bullfeathers; the one who's really something is your partner, you talk more like a politician than a policeman, and the politicians of course owe us big time.

Let's see, Chickenmite, did you see any shadows, hear any voices, did anything catch your attention? Nothing, everything was quiet, once in a while one of the bodyguards of the heavyweights would pass by, but nothing else. Could anyone have dropped the bundle out of a window? No, there are no windows there, they dropped it from the roof, there's no other way. You touched the fabric and it seemed like good material. My 'ama was a seamstress, and as a kid I'd help her cut the fabric, and the soft ones are almost always finer than the rough ones. Right, did you smell it? What are you trying to say, I'm no stoner, I picked it up out of curiosity, to see if somebody was playing a practical joke. What sort of joke? Zelda was watching. Throwing away a guy's uniform, tying the legs in knots, burning holes in it: the bros don't hold back. What time would it have been? you'd already taken the flowers in. Eight o'clock, more or less. Who did you give the roses to? There were two guys standing guard, one of them took them. Have you ever been arrested? Never, I'm an honest man. Well, this might be your chance if you're hiding anything or you're lying. Uh-uh, don't get your back up, badge-buddy, I'm being straight with you. Where do they take the trash? Twice a day a truck comes and they take it to the city dump. Merry Christmas, Chickenmite. Zelda jumped in: Did you see the colour and size of the uniform? Reddish like mine and a normal size, imagine a buddy who's not short and not tall either, and it didn't have any emblems like these, he pointed to the logo and the name of the hotel chain. Do you think he was fat? You think I looked that closely? nope.

With Ortega, they went to take a look at the dumpster and it was big and wide; they stood where Chickenmite had been working, and sure enough it was impossible to see the rooftop. Then they went up and looked at it from above. Ortega dusted for prints, but everything had been waterproofed. We went over the meeting room and it's totally enclosed, not a single window. O.K., Zelda, get the waterproofers to come over, let's find out if they saw anything.

They were two: an old man and a young fellow. There was gar-bage around, but nothing special. We're looking for a thousand-peso bill, have you seen it? The old man said he hadn't. Then it must have been you. Go ahead and frisk me. Oh, yeah? call Chopper in here, the detective asked his partner, then he turned back to the young man: He's our best frisker, you won't believe how he makes you remember things that never even happened. The workers looked at each other. Come on, Octopus, if you got something, tell them or they're going to beat the shit out of you. The young guy looked at Lefty: Chief, I did see something, rather I took something; a pulley and a mechanism for going up and down with a little remote-control motor you can barely hear humming; it was down below, next to the wall, near the dumpster. Did you see it from the roof? Yes. Where is it now? At home.

Chopper walked in. Go get Devil and take this kid to his house, he's going to give you a mechanism for rappelling, make sure it's all there. Minutes later Ortega came over: We're done, all we need is the wire, even if it's full of Jack the Ripper's prints we might find something. Wait for me in the lobby. Lefty went down to Samantha and Mariana's rooms. He went over them carefully once more, they had the usual furnishings and he discovered nothing. The stain on the pillow, no signs of violence. Suppose Samantha killed her? Impossible, I could see the heartache in her eyes; though I'd bet she's incapable of suffering for the dead, at least her father's death didn't seem to affect her; what about Garcés? No, there are dogs that'll die for their masters and he's one of those. He went into the bathroom and again nothing: everything in its place. He went over to the window, confirmed that it was secure. If the murderer rapelled down here and found it open he would have had no problem getting in, especially if Mariana was in the shower; they found her in a bathrobe; suppose the window was closed? The mechanism looks solid. Those gringos are really old and they only go out to take a walk, at that time of day he would have been asleep and she was watching Frank Sinatra. Deaf as she is, she wouldn't have heard a thing and neither of them knew there was a body down the hall. The window only opens from the inside, he tried it. And there were no scratches or signs of forced entry, the murderer also picked up the casing and cartridge. A professional.

Fucking pros, every day they get tougher to crack. He went over each corner of both rooms and gave his imagination a break to recharge. He stood still. He could see the technicians had been everywhere, yet something was floating around that room, something he could not pin down; what was it? No fucking idea.

In the lobby. Let's see, Devil, my friend, your boss was not quite clear enough on one point: was there a meeting of the heavyweights here or something like that? My man Lefty, didn't they tell you? there was a meeting of the kingpins or their lieutenants to see how to handle this business of the war. What kingpins? The ones that make up the Pacific Cartel, it was Saturday at nine, and while the meeting was going on they whacked the señorita. So that's why they pulled you from your wedding. I had to bring the undertakers from San Chelín. Did you see the body? It was face down, covered with a sheet, under the sheet a bathrobe was covering her back from her shoulders to her behind. Did you see the hole in her head? In my opinion it was a .45, right between the eyebrows. Did you see the shell? Not me or anybody else, I'm saying that because I asked; as you can see, I've still got a bit of the badge in me. Lefty wrote the information in his notebook and added: grabbed her, covered her mouth, shot. Did you notice anything unusual about the guards? The one who was slogging the rounds down below was really nervous, I heard Max the boss put the squeeze on him, but maybe he had nothing to do with it, he's kind of slow and he's got lousy aim, a bit of a daydreamer, but he's loyal; he's good with the A.K., you should have seen him that night shooting up those assholes, in fact he tied three of the six that ended up swinging from the bridge. Where is he? In Culiacán. Are you having a good time? Fabulous, my man Lefty, fabulous, by the way, my father-in-law told me you've got yourself a hand brake and she's really hot stuff. Lefty hung his head, Zelda smiled. Devil, spend the night here, and Chopper you too. I can't do that, my man Lefty, I'm to follow you wherever you go. The one giving the orders here is me, didn't Garcés tell you that? Clear as could be, you're in charge. Well, I order you to stay overnight and I want both of you in Culiacán tomorrow at two o'clock. Thank you, my man Lefty, it's obvious you were young once. What, do I look old now, you bastard? You look fine, I'm just saying, what's with the bruises? Ah, I'll tell you later; the iron's hot, Zelda, let's go where they treat us like people. Ortega and his team were waiting in the van.

What was he not seeing?

Thirty

Two black pickups, one pockmarked with bullet-holes, tore down the main street of Aguaruto. The streets were full of people shopping for gifts or a few more lights or tinsel to finish decorating their houses. The trucks screeched to a stop in front of an office with a sign: DR FERNANDO SÁINZ, DENTAL SURGEON, U.N.A.M. Uncle Beto went up to the glass door and rang the bell, but no-one answered. The store next door, a place where people went to get their presents wrapped, was open. Good afternoon, do you know what time the dentist gets in? Ah, señor, he went to Mazatlán on vacation a week ago; he won't be back until January 2; if it's urgent there's another dentist two blocks down, he's my nephew and for sure he'll be there. Do you recommend him? Absolutely, go and you'll see how pleased you'll be, that boy is renowned.

Uncle Beto was driving, Tenia Solium by his side, wasting away. The fuckin' pain is killin' me; I swear if he gives me a good yank I'll let him live. He'll do it for you, boss, he'll do it for you, his aunt told me he was renowned, you'll be free of this torture at last. Fuckin' whore of a mother, I never felt so rotten, Uncle Beto, and all for a fuckin' skanky tooth. Some body parts are a bitch, aren't they? In the back, Valentillo was concentrating on the sign he was finishing, which he planned to leave on the next body: *For a rat / kidz, dont be jackin cars.*

Soon they reached the dentist's office, but it was also closed.

Uncle Beto asked a woman selling fruit and vegetables nearby. The dentist? no, I haven't seen him, he must be in Culiacán; he likes to bend his elbow and sometimes he stays drunk for a week, it's only been three days this time. Where does he live? But he's not home, he's my brother-in-law, that's how I know he's in Culiacán in some cantina drinking beer. Do you know which cantina? He'll duck into the first one he finds, he's got no taste, and he won't leave until they throw him out; my poor sister, he's made her look her fate in the face.

Boss, if we find that drunk bastard, we'll whack him. O.K., Uncle Beto, but first he's got to yank this fuckin' molar. I've got the sign ready, 'apa. On the kerb, two kids dressed as Santa Claus were playing cowboys. Christmas was here.

Thirty-One

César tried to cheer Luigi up: he threw him balls, gave him food, offered him bones, but nothing worked; he jumped up and down and yelled in his face, and the dog remained unmoved. Luigi wouldn't eat, every day the bodyguards brought him something, stews or croquettes, but he never touched them; he looked thin, sad, feeble, only the door to the street drew his attention. He was waiting. One of the young guys thought he would never recover and murmured that they should put a bullet in him: So the poor fellow won't suffer. He was advised not to mention it again. In the kitchen Samantha's cell rang; she was helping her mother prepare an asado sinaloense. At that moment she was pouring hot water on slices of red onion to rid them of the smell, before washing them with cool water and squeezing on fresh lime juice. Talk to me, Lefty Mendieta, she pulled a Romaine lettuce out of the refrigerator. No, better you talk to me: how big was the meeting at the hotel? She put the lettuce on the table. It was a meeting of the group, I don't want my people getting involved in the war and I've got to remind them all the time that we're traffickers not murderers. You'll agree with me that it's a universe of potential suspects. Forget it, they're all trustworthy and they were all at the meeting. How much time went by between the moment you left Mariana in her room and when you sat down with the bros? A good while, maybe an hour, I was on the phone with my son, then I showered and did a few other things. That's a long time, Samantha, I've got to interrogate those bastards. Impossible. Then I can't continue. He could hear the sizzling of hot oil. This has got to stay confidential, Lefty, and as I already told you, I don't believe any of them did it. If you won't help me I can't bring you the culprit. But it wasn't any of them, I'm certain, we were all together. But not at that time, understand me. You understand *me*, if I stop trusting my people I'm done for, is there anything else you want? No, we're finished here; by the way, thank you for the present. You're welcome, now you know you're appreciated. She hung up. César, who was playing by himself, ran past her spitting out threats against imaginary enemies: You're going to die, your picture will be in the papers tomorrow. Minerva sliced the radishes, chopped up the squash and the parboiled potatoes, took the boiled meat out of the pot to cut into cubes, and all the while Samantha barely washed the lettuce. If you want my advice, let him talk to them; if that policeman agreed to work with you, I don't think he would do it in bad faith. Mama, then he'll know who's who and he won't forget. I know, but if he needs to see them to find Mariana's murderer, I think you ought to run the risk; don't forget what happened to us with Eloy Quintana, he betrayed us and he was the man your father trusted most, what can you expect of a horde of lieutenants, which is who you said went to the meeting? They fell silent. Samantha cut the lettuce into strips, and her mother put the cubes of meat into a pan so they could fry while she was cutting up the cooked carrots. The one I feel sorry for is the widow, but what could we do? Just show her a little respect, Ma, should we put sour cream on it? It tastes better with fresh cheese and a bit of agua de jamaica. Mariana once told me that's good for your cholesterol. Yes, she knew about those things, have you got any avocados? No, I don't think so. Now that I can hardly believe. Daughter, with so much going on I don't even know where my head is.

Samantha picked up her cell and called the detective back. Alright, Lefty Mendieta, I'll get in touch with my partners, anything else? Did any of them bring someone along? No, we asked them to come alone and Max Garcés made sure that's the way it was; and as soon as the meeting was over they all took off. Later on I might need to know more about one or another, of course I'll let you contact them. Thank you, Lefty Mendieta. O.K., we're going to get something to eat. Go to El Chuchupetas in Villa Unión. What do you think of Chon in downtown Mazatlán? The last thing I'd expect is that you'd like my father's favourite restaurant. Your father was a legend, Samantha. What do you mean a legend? We'll talk about that some other time, see you later. Don't forget that Christmas is less than a week away. Are you sure it happened while you were at the meeting? Absolutely, that's why it couldn't be any of them; she ground black pepper and sprinkled it on the meat juices which they would use for dressing. Do you remember what time you last saw her? A little after seven, we got back from the beach and each of us went into our rooms, I called my son, I got ready and I went to the meeting, it would have been about eight, eight-twenty maybe, when I joined the group. Pardon me, but you didn't sleep in the same room? Sure, but I always keep a room next door for receiving people or giving orders, and to be by myself;

of course I could have showered in hers, but this time I didn't. Did you hear any sounds outside? it looks like the murderer slid down from the roof before eight o'clock. Really? the bastard, he was stalking us; I didn't hear a thing, Lefty Mendieta, I was talking with my son, a really long call, and then I showered quickly, my hair was full of sand. Do you have any idea who might hate her that much? Her? impossible, nobody; me, more people than I could ever recall. We were told the bodyguards were seen doing their rounds. They were all our people, no-one brought their own protection to the hotel; beyond the grounds we can't control, more than a few of them think they're being followed everywhere. Some of the hotel workers mentioned a meeting of the heavy-weights, wasn't it a secret? Well, look, after this tragedy I don't know anymore. O.K., I'll call you later. Enjoy your meal.

Samantha and Minerva served the food.

Thirty-Two

Boss, I have to tell you something. They had already rung up three plates of shrimp plus an octopus-and-conch appetiser, along with several cold Pacíficos. Everyone looked at Zelda, who then filled them in on Gori's encounter with Constantino Blake Hernández. Seriously? Someone beat up Gori? Introduce me to him. Poor Gori, who would have thought. The years are catching up with him. Hey, hey, he's no older than any of us, Ortega defended him, his team of technicians smiled. We have to do something. And then what happened? We went shopping at the Forum, Angelita, Gori and I. What! Gori shopping at the Forum? that is serious. Could he be turning queer? Of course not, what does it matter if he goes to buy a gift? These are strange times we're living through, this bastard turns up with a son exactly like him, then Gori gets beat up and goes shopping. And the boss gets a souvenir in the eye. It's Christmas, anything can happen. The way you tell it, it doesn't seem normal to me. That's without counting what we were just up to. "Christmas time is here, happiness and cheer," the singing technician piped up. Does my daughter ever drive me nuts with that song. What should we do for Gori? Let him retire. Hey, easy, he said that yesterday, but last night he didn't mention it. Tell us what he bought. A girdle. A red thong. Don't be nasty, he bought a couple of T-shirts for himself, a bottle of perfume for his wife and another for his daughter. Good idea, the perfume, I've got to get my old lady something. He also bought a present for you, boss. Oh yeah? what is it? Alright, I'll tell you, but don't you let on: a book. Gori bought me a book? For sure it's that bestseller, the one with poems for reading out loud. Wrong, Chief Ortega, it's a novel. I can't believe Gori knows what a novel is. Well, he asked the bookseller, remember he's no dummy. Leave my friend alone, you fucking loco. Aren't you the greedy one, fucking Lefty. It's Christmas, asshole. "Christmas time is here, happiness and cheer." They ate grilled fish, breaded shrimp and ordered more beer. As far as I know Gori has never given anything to anybody, not even at the Secret Santa. Fucking Lefty, you're screwing him or what? Hey, hey, I'm right here. Forgive me, Zelda, forgive me. What's the novel? *The Count of Monte Cristo*. Is it thick? Fucking Ortega, don't ask stupid questions. For sure it's a comic book. Your mother, asshole. Señores, Zelda banged her beer with a spoon, I asked you a question: What can we do for Gori? do you have any ideas? One. Well, tell us. "Christmas time is here, happiness and cheer." Shut up with that fucking song or I'll bust your nuts, jerkoff. Hey, what's wrong with you, embrace the season. Agreed, Zelda my dear, but keep this faggot from singing, I put up with it from my little girl, but there's no reason I have to listen to him. Don't fuck with me, you bastard, it's no big deal. Fucking Gori. Well, we've got work to do in Culichi, shall we go? What about dessert? Ask for the cheque. And what about Gori? Yeah, I'll tell you about my idea in the car. He could become a monk. He could open a school for torturers. We should hang out for a while. Impossible, we have work in Navolato. Don't be a jerk, this isn't any old place, it's Mazatlán, the pearl of the Pacific. Sure is filled with great-looking women. And faggots. That's what you really want, isn't it, asshole? Hey, please, a little respect, I'm not a blow-up doll. It's ten past six. "Silent Night, Holy Night." *The Count of Monte Cristo*, you say? there's no fixing you, when you want to gossip, nobody can stop you. Don't tell on me, boss, eh?

Susana flooded his mind: everybody loved her; that time she asked me about books I wanted to impress her and I thought I could do it by playing the tough guy; that's why I told her I never read love stories; *The Count*, it's not really about vengeance, it's a love story like the one rolling around my brain these days; what did I see and not see in that hotel room that would give us something to go on? On the car stereo: José Alfredo's "Ojalá que Te Vaya Bonito". Maybe they've invented bullets that go through walls and windows without making a hole, they zoom around and find the victim, whack him and make their way calmly back to the pistol; well, why not? it couldn't have been the invisible man.

Suppose I ask her to stay? Yes! Take it easy, fucking body, who asked you to butt in? Well, I did; you don't think it's your astonishing intelligence that's got her all worked up? no, señor; admit it, I'm the draw, and even though I'm convalescing I miss her. Enough, asshole, leave me in peace. Don't pull out. Don't butt in. Ay.

Thirty-Three

María Leyva, blonde and thin, strong, hair pulled back, small breasts, entered the bedroom where Ugarte was fiddling with the Bible: he would open it at random, read the first few lines and imagine it said something about his future or the future of his family or friends; "I am come into my garden / my sister, my spouse / I have gathered my myrrh / with my spice / I have eaten my honeycomb with my honey / I have drunk my wine with my milk." Yes, I am come, I have come, I've lived the life I was born into, and whatever happens I shall be with her and she shall be with me; none of it was easy: not the College, not my profession, certainly not my family life. There's nothing simple about living with a lesbian, too many days filled with uncertainty, contrary lusts, insomniac nights; in fact I'll never forgive her that. Why did we marry? me, because I adored her and she never insisted I be at home, not even when the children were born; she, for my feminine soul; she always said that: You are a beautiful and delicate woman with a penis; I don't know why you aren't a homosexual. He was lying on three pillows. His skin had grown even more pallid and scaly and he weighed less each day. Dear, two señores are here to see you, I told them you're not well enough to see anyone, but they insist. Who are they? They say they don't carry cards and I didn't ask them their names because I didn't think they would tell me the truth. He was going to ask her to try to convince them, that he just did not have the energy, when the two crossed the threshold into the bedroom and one glance was enough to know what it was about. He had never seen them before, but they had the sinister air of impious men. Señora, do us the favour of stepping outside. María looked at him, he nodded and shifted on the pillows. The one who had spoken came a little closer. Héctor Ugarte, nice house, and a pretty wife, eh, and everybody knows you don't go for that. He felt a twinge, placed the Bible on his chest, coughed lightly. What can I do for you? For us, nothing, and from what I can see nothing for yourself either. He observed them: they wore grey suits and dark ties; dark-skinned, stone-faced, elegant. I'm dying. We know, and people who care about you decided to save you the suffering. A murderer who speaks too much is either afraid or a cynic, or he wants to humiliate. He shifted again on the pillows and in the same movement pulled out a Glock 34 and drilled each of them. María Leyva, who was waiting behind the door with a Sig Sauer P226 in her fist, burst into the bedroom, thinking it was he who had been shot. She contemplated the scene with a wry smile, disarmed the visitors, one dead and one mortally wounded, and asked: Now what? Ugarte was sweating, his eyes closed, his gun hand on the covers. Where's Francelia? She's with friends. Call her, tell her to meet us in Mexico City, tell her to take a taxi to the U.N.A.M. and wait for us at the entrance to the campus, near the School of Philosophy and Letters, on Universidad Avenue; tell her to bring her passport and whatever cash she has. He sat up with difficulty. Help me get dressed. Whatabout them? Someone will be along soon enough to get them.

They parked their car at a supermarket open twenty-four hours and took a taxi to the capital, seventy kilometres away. She had asked only one question: Who were they? While he guessed they might be envoys from the Secretary or the narcos, he said I have no idea; he detested the former, who had plenty of power and kept his subordinates elegantly dressed; the latter were sworn enemies and now they were at war; although, truth be told, they knew little of him, he was from another epoch, and besides, thanks to the disguise and his thinness he was sure no-one had recognised him at the meeting. The army? no, it's an institution that never betrays its members; as soon as he was near a telephone he would call General Alvarado, since he knew his own must be tapped. Now all that mattered was to get his family to safety, his son was still in New York seeing musicals, so he was in no immediate danger; he had to get Francelia out of the country, and María could go into hiding with him until the disease finished him off or he followed through with military tradition and put a bullet in his head. Could it be the new group the General mentioned? If it was, why would they come for me when I'm on my last legs? So much for comfort, maybe it makes sense to go back to the old house in Culiacán, since it looks abandoned it would be perfect for hiding out. He realised he did not want to fight, he just wanted to die in his own bed on the day his body gave up or when he gave it the little push it needed. In all honesty, he was still not sure which he preferred; we Catholics take our end very seriously.

Cold. The cab-driver turned off the Christmas music and soon they were on the highway lined with pines. It was dark when they entered the city, coloured lights everywhere. They spied Francelia where they expected her, by the entrance to the National University, which was closed for the vacation. She got into the taxi without asking a thing, but she looked upset, her lips were trembling when she kissed them. She was wearing black: stockings, short skirt, blouse and coat. Are you alright? *Yes*, in English. At the Gandhi bookstore they changed cabs. Before that, Ugarte explained the situation and the next steps. The young woman broke down and sobbed silently: Again? can't we be together even in your final days? well, I disagree, I'm going with you to Culiacán, if you're going to be safe there, so will I. Maybe it's just an obsession of mine, but something in my gut tells me you ought to be with your brother to protect him. His voice breaking. Aramís can protect himself, Pa, in Manhattan he barely sleeps, you know he wants to direct musicals, he's seeing two a day; so, shall we go by way of Toluca or Querétaro, or are we flying out from Benito Juárez? Let's go by Toluca, tomorrow we'll look for a flight from the airport in Guadalajara. But you're sick. Sure, but I'm still here and that's something. They hugged each other.

An hour later they crossed under the Periférico Highway in a white minivan with Tlaxcala plates.

Thirty-Four

Navolato. City of farmers, shopkeepers, a sugar refinery, and in La Flor de Capomo no women allowed. What? Just the way you heard it, señor, the waiter told Lefty, the señora has to go. Hey, you should be talking to me, Zelda protested, her voice rising, I'm the one you're dealing with, now get me your boss. They were at a table with wooden chairs in a nasty-smelling cantina. Señora, I don't want any trouble, I can't serve you. What kind of fucking town is this where they still discriminate against women? It's the rule, besides, soon the boys will start acting out, thinking you're something else. On the sound system "Mujeres Divinas" by Vicente Fernández. Call the owner, a frankly irritated Mendiata cut in. I can't serve you. You already said that, now go get the boss. A dozen little red bells hanging from the walls signalled that the year was drawing to a close. The bartender put a few frosted mugs on the wooden bar, along with several open bottles of beer. Everyone in the room was watching attentively, most of them working men in search of a bit of cheap entertainment. And while you're at it, bring out José Rodelo. The waiter, a puny man wearing an apron with pockets for napkins and the money he collected from customers, yelled something toward the back and hurried to carry the mugs to their destination. They were seated near the entrance.

A fat man with a chip on his shoulder approached the table. Señor, this business has rules, and number one is that women are not allowed. That is vile discrimination. It's the way it is, señora, and we're also violating the Mexican Constitution, but there's no fixing it here; La Flor de Capomo is Comanche territory, or what amounts to the same thing: the land of men. Well, you're going to serve me a beer. Not even if you people are from the Interior Ministry and are going to shutter the business for the rest of my life. What do you have against women? Me? nothing, God forbid, it's simply the way things are here; look at it like this: my wife has a beauty salon and she doesn't take care of men or faggots, only women; one day Carmen Aristegui and Javier Solórzano came in here and Carmen had to wait outside. A furious Zelda turned to Mendieta. Can we go to your office?

Once they were all inside a room filled with kitchen utensils and spicy aromas: You're badges, right? We want to talk to the Glasseater, not long ago they killed his dentist and he was his last patient. The fat man looked at them: He's a good boy, sit down, he indicated two empty plastic chairs; he's about to do his number, as soon as he finishes I'll send him in to you. Could you bring or send in a couple of beers? Zelda insisted. Your tongues are parched, aren't they? if you like, you can watch the show through there, he pointed to a small window in the fibreboard wall.

Background music: Steppenwolf's "Born to be Wild".

Good evening, dear friends, welcome to your fayvorritte barr.

Oh yeah, it's me, candy-asses, don't throw a fit.

(Boos and whistles.)

What was that you said? it's Burro Van Rankin in his underwear, right? Uh-uh, not him or his mother; it's me.

We thought it was your whore of a mother.

Enough, fucking impotents, take it easy; it's obvious you left your women wanting more; but no need to worry, your good buddy is here and he won't leave you high and dry.

Shut the fuck up, you smug bastard.

You're a faggot.

La Flor de Capomo bar has the pleasure of presenting

In exclusive engagement

The only man on the terrestrial sphere who has found the solution to world hunger

Directly from Las Vegas, Nevada

The famous

Glasseater!

(More boos and whistles.)

A heavyset man, twenty-seven years old, dressed in blue, appeared with three half-drunk beers in his hands. He drank one down. You're thirsty, fucking Glasseater. Drink water, asshole, leave the beer for the men. Rodelo bit off the neck of the bottle he had emptied and chewed slowly, as if he were demonstrating how it ought to be done. He used a microphone and everyone could hear the shards grinding. Crinch crunch. That's stale bread you're swallowing, Glasseater, you're not fooling us, here's a real one for you, the protesting customer heaved a litre bottle, which Rodelo caught on the fly, then bit off the neck and chewed hungrily. Crinch crunch. They brought him one of tequila and same story: impassive and deliberate grinding to the violent rhythms of Hermann Hesse's Canadian fans. For eleven minutes he chewed glass to the delight of the audience and the astonishment of the detectives. The bastard's crazy. Soon they were sending him full bottles without a pause in their shouts: Come here and bite what's hanging from me, fucking Glasseater, let's see if you dare.

Good evening again, candy-asses.

How about a round of applause for the Glasseater

And his world-famous show!

The music rose, Rodelo departed amid loud whistles and the odd flying bottle.

He went to join the detectives, carrying three beers. Good evening, he handed a bottle to each and drank his own in one guzzle. Ahhh, there are those who praise the first sip, but for me it's all the same. For us too, listen, what's the trick? He bit off a chunk of his bottle and chewed gently. The glass in his mouth crunched loudly, you could hear it getting ground up, and once it was reduced to a powder he swallowed it. Good answer. Rodelo smiled. Saliva, mine is thicker than most people's, but every once in a while a shard sticks in my gums. That's why you went to Dr Antonio Estolano, may he rest in peace. Tell us what you saw, we heard you were his last patient. The dentist was a good guy, he must have been about seventy, he pulled out the glass and was done in five minutes, didn't want to charge me a thing; he took off his coat right away because he wanted to watch a football match on television; I hurried out and that was it, a few days later I heard somebody took him down. You've got an interesting way of earning a living, I imagine you get paid well. I'm happy with it, the drunks never let me down, I pass the hat and they cooperate. But you get a salary too. A hundred pesos a day. You live with your wife and three small children and you're from a little town called La Pipima. Rodelo smiled: I left high school because I got sick and tired of going to class without breakfast. I'm glad we understand each other, what did you see when you left Dr Estolano's office? Not even his receptionist because she'd already gone. We've never had a glass eater in Aguaruto Prison, would you like to be the first? You're going to throw me in the slammer so soon? Who did you see? Well, I'm going to tell you, but promise me if they come for me the government will take care of my children, as you know I've got three. First thing tomorrow morning I'll send you an insurance agent. Don't make fun of me, I don't want my kids to be worth shit like me, I want them to become professionals. Señor Rodelo, if something happens to you, I'll take care of them, proposed Zelda, only give me your word you won't go around flapping your gums or taunting your enemies; you stay home until we solve this mess, agreed? Better you take me with you to Culiacán, I'd like to do a show at El Quijote, they say it's a great bar, the bros there are really wild. Done deal. He smiled, his teeth were crooked but they looked strong. When I left the office, two black pickups arrived, I crossed the street but I managed to see several gunslingers get out, one of them was a guy who's famous, they call him Tenia Solium and he had his head tied up with a cloth, the way you do when your tooth hurts; I moved off a ways, saw the dentist come out, they spoke with him, he looked at his watch and shook his head; then Tenia put the barrel on him, they piled him into one of the trucks and took him away; end of story. Wait, describe Tenia Solium. He's hefty, not very tall, dark-skinned, short hair, and he controls the highway between Culiacán and Navolato. Does he have a house around here? No, not that I know of, I think the dude is from the hills; he runs a really bloody gang; I've dealt with most of the narcos from around here, they like to see me eat glass and they treat me well, I'm finishing a house with what they've paid me; if he lived around here I'd know about it. Does he have a family? Couldn't say. Cavalry charge: Mendieta, the detective answered. It was Quiroz. Inkshitter, where have you been hiding, you fucking sell-out? Hey, I went to Colombia to take a course at Gabriel García Márquez's New Journalism Foundation. Seriously? gee, I thought they didn't accept primates. So soon, my man Lefty? don't be riding me, you ought to know that's a serious crime. My, didn't you come back all delicate, did the narcos down there beat the shit out of you, or what? That I'll tell you about later, listen, what do you make of this wave of dentist murders? Not bad, two down so far, one of whom was yours. I know, I need information. Go to the chief, yesterday he told me he missed you, he didn't think he could have a merry Christmas without you. Before you go on fucking with me, I brought you a present, it's instant coffee. You think I'm going to drink your poison? you're dreaming, inkshitter. I'll look for you tomorrow.

At 11.00 they got on the highway to Culiacán.

Thirty-Five

At a safe house in the neighbourhood of Las Quintas he met up with Max Garcés. Samantha Valdés gave me the list of the people at the Mazatlán meeting, was it you who made the reservations? Max Garcés smiled: P.C. did. The Pacific Cartel, I know, did you assign them rooms or was it first-come first-served? We handed out the keys as each arrived. Did all of them come alone? We checked that very carefully, no-one brought a companion or a bodyguard, most of them arrived a little before the meeting and left when it ended. Were they people you knew? Four of them. Are there new people all the time? Ever since the war began, they're never the same. Do you remember how the rooms were distributed? We were on either side, above, below and across from the señoras, two on the first floor, four on the second and two on the third; the women were on the second floor, surrounded, and there were a couple of doddering gringos at the end we couldn't evict. Were any of your men in either of the women's rooms when they did the deed? No, not then, we were in the hallways and the garden outside, I gave you the video, remember, you can see the dude watching the señorita's hallway in his position, we call him the Bogeyman, and you can see the gringos coming back from a stroll. Lefty had watched the video but seen nothing worth noting. There aren't any exterior cameras, but Drysnot was keeping watch out there. Who's half blind, Devil told me. Not so blind he wouldn't see somebody approaching. We found evidence the murderer rappelled down from the roof and came in the window, what's the exterior lighting like? Max grew thoughtful. A little weak, in those hotels that's how they do it. He used a uniform the same colour as the wall and similar to the ones the workers wear and he must have done it so quickly and silently your guard didn't notice. I'm not surprised, he's really young, maybe some gringas in thongs walked by and he got a little distracted. Max scratched behind his ear. The reason the murderer could be connected to your group is he knew Mariana was in her room, what time did the señoras arrive from Culiacán? We got to the hotel at five, before that we ate at El Cuchupetas. Did you have people in the rooms before? From the moment they gave them to us. We have a list of when each of your guests got in and it looks like they came between two and five in the afternoon, do you remember who was in which room? We never pay attention to that and no-one writes it down. Tell me their approximate ages. Most between forty and sixty, the youngest is from Ciudad Juárez, probably thirty-nine, and the oldest is from Tijuana, about seventy. Did you notice anything unusual in the room where the murder took place, something you hadn't seen when you inspected it? Nothing, I'm even surprised about the window, we thought it was secure; the señorita likes to keep her window open, but she was told to keep it closed when she wasn't standing by it and she obeyed the rules. Did anyone arrive early, maybe the day before or in the morning? No, everyone came after two; I should have put someone on the roof. Did he really come from there, Lefty wondered, or was he trying to throw us off the trail? O.K., now bring in the guard who won the booby prize.

It could have been a boy-girl team, maybe the girl wearing a dental-floss thong distracted the guard while the guy slid down and managed to get in the window somehow. Like in the movies, she could have sashayed up to the guard, a cigarette between her red lips, asking for a light, the kid pulls out a lighter and ogles her tits while he lights the cigarette. Still flirting she blows smoke in his face and wiggles her breasts. I like that, fucking Lefty, you're thinking about how hot the dames are. You again? You know I'm only now recovering from the thrashing the gringo gave me, as a matter of fact I was glad to hear how it affected his health. Enough, we'll go and see Susana soon. There's a man for you, not a piece of shit.

I'm Drysnot. Your name. That's it. Don't be a jerk, tell me your name, the one your parents gave you. Cayetano Villa Solano. What's wrong with you? Nothing. Stop pretending this isn't about you, I know you have problems with your eyesight. A little, when it's getting dark and there isn't much light, my eyes go wonky. Does it last long? A little while. Where precisely were you standing guard when Mariana Kelly was killed? Do you know the place? Tell me how far you were from the rubber tree. Drysnot looked at the floor. I was under it for a while, then I made my rounds. The murderer slid down from the roof, did you ever look up there? In truth, I didn't. He began to sweat copiously. And you didn't hear the sound of anyone sliding down either. There were some really noisy tourists drinking beer about ten metres away. Men or women? Most of them babes, they were listening to music in English and dancing. Mendieta wrote something in his notebook.

How hot were they? Fuck, they were really good, he mumbled. Wet T-shirts? Forget T-shirts, a few didn't even have underwear. Room with green easy chairs, window with thick glass, the light flooding in. You're afraid they'll kill you, right, asshole? you're shitting yourself. I was born to die, Mr Fuzz, but I can't deny I feel like shit, there are moments I think I'm already dead. I won't tell your boss any of this, so take it easy, maybe it's still not time for you to hang up your sneakers. Thank you, and if you don't have any more questions, I'd like to go, I don't feel well. Are you planning to put a bullet in your head? That's what I deserve, even if they clear all this up it'll never be the same for me. I was told you've been really wild on this latest killing spree. That's my job and yessir, there's a really big demon eating at my insides. Don't kill yourself yet, I've got a couple of questions to ask you another day. Come for me anytime. Hang in there, if you don't I'll tell Max you're the culprit. Not even if God wills it, I'll wait until you don't need me anymore, and right now I'm going to the bathroom. I'm a witness.

Before heading off to find Samantha, he spoke with the Bogey-man, who like Drysnot had not heard a sound, much less a gunshot from the room. No-one was in the rooms on either side, the one on the fourth floor was occupied by a Canadian couple, why didn't he rappel down from there? Because the cameras in the hallways would have caught him, he knew the place; I'll have to take another look at the videos. Ortega still didn't have his report ready. He kept turning it over in his mind as he drove toward Lomas de San Miguel: It could have been any of the guests, especially the eight attendees; loyalty ain't what it used to be, we'll have to look at their histories, see who would have been most likely to betray Samantha. If they were the only ones who knew about the meeting, someone must have hired a professional, those assholes always make us look our fate in the face, fucking faggots; of course, the jerk went up the elevator dressed as a worker, saw that Drysnot was drooling over the naked tourists, slid down, opened the window, went in right when Mariana was coming out of the shower all wet, maybe she was drying her hair, he put a bullet between her eyes, laid her face down; if they found her right away they would think she was sleeping; it could be he killed her in . . . no, for sure she had already come out of the bathroom. How did he open the window? I tried it and it was pretty firm. While Samantha and the others talked about their shit, he slipped out calm as could be the same way he came in; of course, he knew the Bogeyman was in the hallway and that he would be taped there. Then he probably let himself down to the ground and Drysnot ogling the babes thought he was a hotel employee. Too bad they don't have cameras outside or in the bedrooms. Maybe he knocked her off while Samantha was talking with her son, I'll ask Zelda to go through the videos. He dialled her.

Boss, the chief is looking for you. I'll be there in an hour, do we have anything from Ortega? Nothing, he must be knee-deep in cadavers, did you see how many bodies turned up this morning? No. Twenty-six, two or three with narcograms on them. Oh boy. The one who's really heavy is Tenia Solium, Pineda sent me a report on him that's terrifying. We'll talk about that later, tell me, was there anything in Mariana Kelly's room that caught your attention?

179

Boss, I'm working on that, there was something, it's eating at me, I don't know if it was in the room or on the roof, and I can't put my finger on it. It might have been a hitman hired by someone in the group. Since they were the only ones who knew the day, hour and place, that would make sense. Almost, think harder and see if you can figure it out, I'm like you. Should I call Ortega? Don't even think about it, he'd fly off the handle and we wouldn't see the report until next year; I want to take a look at the names of the other guests again, especially the ones staying upstairs. I went over them already, nothing but old folks with arthritis. The videos from the hotel are on my desk, they're labelled by floor, could you take a look at them? Sure. O.K., I'll see you in a little while.

Obregón Avenue was all decked out for Christmas.

Devil said it was a .45. I didn't smell anything funny; well, it was a little more than a week after the murder, and I'm no dog. Did the murderer know they were going to waterproof the roof? No point asking Samantha which of her enemies would want to make her a widow a second time, she's got too many; well, why not?

Before receiving Edgar Mendieta, the head of the Pacific Cartel met with a green-eyed fortune teller who said Mariana's murderer was a man and probably someone she did not know. Is he very strong? King of spades, Señora Valdés, practically invincible, only another king of spades could handle him. Does he live nearby? That information I'm not getting, only that it is a powerful man. You mean he'll strike again? That's possible, the king of spades never rests. Well, neither does the king of coins, we'll see whose skin makes more belts, like my father used to say.

What have you got for me, Lefty Mendieta? We've got something, but first tell me why you haven't eased off on the killings. There are demons on the loose and plenty of bullets to be shot. I thought you could control them. I'd love to, but not all of them live in my hell; besides, the young punks are running free and loving it. I'd like you to do something about it. Don't be ingenuous, not even the President asks me that. That's because he goes around in an armoured car and I don't think he hears as many screams as we do. She smiled. I never thought you would take an interest in the war. Now who's being ingenuous? as far as I'm concerned they can slice each other to bits; all I care about is having a quiet Christmas, for the first time in my life I'm thinking of buying presents. Well, where are we at? We think it was a solitary assassin who rappelled down from the roof and came in the window; we're waiting on the ballistics report; do you suspect any of your enemies? No matter how I look at it, I can't think of anybody who'd have the balls to do something so outrageous. Any suitors? It's been a long time since I've seen any men showing interest, and I'd know about it since they always try to make a big splash. Anyone she dumped? There are lots of those, but none of them would dare go this far, they might pull her hair, but that's about it; Mariana was reading a book by Mónica Lavín, I looked through it and there's nothing underlined or anything else that might indicate she was afraid, will it be of any use? Later on you can lend it to me, I want you to call the people who were at the meeting from a telephone where I can listen in. My cell has a speaker. Perfect, I know only lieutenants came, do you have their numbers? and then I'll tell you who I want to see here; how far in advance did they know the place and time of the meeting? Three days. That much? They needed to take precautions for travelling, especially in the current circumstances. O.K. They called Max who came in with the list.

You are going to ask each of them for the name of the person they came with. They came alone. No matter, and if Max does the talking, all the better. Garcés telephoned the first. What's up, Chávez, this is Max Garcés, how's Juaritos? Hey, Max, great to hear from you, how's the fuse in Culichi? Burning, my man Chávez, and you? On my toes, following La Jefa's instructions and drinking like a fish, somebody gave me a case of Mexican wine that's dynamite. Strange you like it better than beer, listen, what's the name of that person you brought with you to Mazatlán? You know I was hot to take a babe along, but I went alone, those were the orders, weren't they? You didn't even bring bodyguards? Nothing. Great, we'll be seeing you. O.K., my man Max.

They all answered more or less the same until they got to Mexicali.

Thirty-Six

María Leyva was at the wheel of the white minivan, deftly handling the traffic, Francelia asleep at her side; in the back, stretched out on seats converted into a bed, Héctor Ugarte remained awake. They were on the highway to Guadalajara. By now they must have figured out they didn't get me, for sure they're running around like crazy looking for us, they've probably torn the house down, broken everything we have and got the neighbours all upset; who were they? was the Secretary mad enough to send his men in grey suits? what a nefarious jerk, he doesn't know how to wield power. I bet he was hoping I would call General Alvarado, but he was wrong, his telephones must be tapped like mine. He recognised Glenn Miller's "American Patrol", which María had on to keep drowsiness at bay. Maybe not, more likely he would have sent one of the bodyguards I'd met to humiliate me; so? From the moment I laid eyes on him in the Hilton he gave me a bad feeling. Yet sometimes an idea can suddenly become so urgent you draw on everything you've got to pull it off; but why am I avoiding thinking about it? He felt slightly nauseous and a wave of pain swept through him, paralysing him for a moment. This isn't any old thing, and you're no champion without a trophy, who said dying would be easy? He resisted the urge to moan so as not to upset his wife, who believed the movement of the car was bound to make him feel sicker and even suggested they stay in some nondescript hotel. When you're on the run nothing is secure and no place is nondescript, there are informers everywhere. The narcos? no, I don't think so, they would have massacred everyone in the house and wouldn't have given me the chance to fire; Alvarado thinks a new group is being formed, an elite corps, but these seemed like novices, they let me surprise them; I was part of an elite corps, and frankly it's something else, those boys seemed like dimwits. Do you want me to take a turn? he heard Francelia. Are you feeling alright? Uh-huh, I had a nap, how's Pa? Asleep, he hasn't complained; at the next tollbooth or gas station we can trade places, are you sure you're up for it? *Yes*, in English. *Oui*, in French. They smiled. Ugarte in the back enjoyed their chatter. That's why I won't let them kill me; I'm going to die, no way around it, but I want to spend the days I have left with these two. If my son is going to musicals in New York, he'll be fine; he could have been a cyclist and competed in the Tour de France, but everybody chooses the cross they'll bear for the rest of their lives. Sometimes mine was light, though most of the time it was just the opposite, insufferable; María, you owe me more kisses than all the grains of sand on the beach at Altata, you can't imagine what I've done for your love; my profession did not make me happy, I understand that now, I can see anonymity doesn't suit me; I would have liked everyone to know who I am, to have known of my skills, what I've achieved, how I've managed to make a family with this difficult and incredible woman; where will we end up? Killing is easy, but dying is something else; now I know we won't be safe in Culiacán either. Zzz. He drowsily caressed the Smith & Wesson in his hand. Zzz.

Bit by bit, zzz, he was falling into the zzz, pool of zzz.

At Guadalajara Airport María waited in line for tickets to Culiacán. "Customer Juan Nepomuceno Pérez Vizcaíno, passenger on flight 1955 for Comala, please come to gate number thirty-eight, your flight is departing." Francelia was buying a few things for herself and oral rehydration salts for her father. It was seven o'clock in the morning, they had slept in the van, where Ugarte was now sweating and waiting. Everywhere, more Christmas decorations and ambient Christmas music. The saleswomen worked slowly, almost sleepily, and María wanted everything sped up so she could go see if her husband needed the bathroom or had thrown up.

That was when she saw them. There were two: young, muscular, shorn heads, the same attitude as the ones they had left lying on her floor. My God. She spotted Francelia, who already had the salts, a bag of potato chips and a red Gatorade, and she waved at her to head in the other direction. Like in a movie, the girl pretended to be looking at magazines and then bought a newspaper. The men continued watching unperturbed, impassive. Grey suits, dark neckties. María remained in line, a line that was not quite crowded enough for her to disappear without calling attention to herself. At the counter she asked for flights to New York. There was a plane leaving at one in the afternoon. Do you have nine seats? I'm sorry, there are only three left and they're not together, the rest of the group will have to go at eight tonight. Let me ask them, would you like me to go back to the end of the line? No, just come right to me, I'll give you twenty minutes. Thank you. She walked slowly toward the exit. Her cell rang but she did not answer. She spied another pair of men at the door by which she would have left, looking very much like the first, and she spotted her daughter in a crowd walking to the parking lot. Cold. Overcast.

What should we do? Don't forget my medicine. The young woman turned to face her father, who had been interrogating them. Pa, we're surrounded, let's go on by land, do you think you can make it? María turned her head, calm but running on adrenaline. Let's do that, you'll be safer there. We could stay near here. Mazamitla, Ma, we haven't been there in such a long time. If they're in the airport, they'll soon be on the highway, let's get ahead of them; from what you're telling me, they don't think we're leaving from here, they're expecting us to arrive, let's take advantage of that, he recalled that the Secretary thought he lived in Guadalajara. How long has it been since we last travelled to Culiacán by land? Eighty years. Are you sure they aren't already there? No, I'm not sure of anything anymore. It's true, our odds are shrinking. And my aunt sold her place in the country last year. So? Let's trust in "The Purloined Letter" effect. Pa, that was in the nineteenth century, Edgar Allan Poe wouldn't know which way was up today. You'd be surprised at the things that don't change. I hope this is one of them; can I know why they're after you like this? Please, Francelia. Let her, María, she's part of the picture now; daughter, I am a small enemy of a very powerful person. But who is it, who could be so influential as to mount this operation to keep you from ending your days peacefully or even take a plane? what did you do to make them hunt you down like this? María did not try to stop him from answering. There are three or four people it could be. Is one of them the person you went to see in Mexico City a little while ago? That's likely. Héctor, you should tell us so we know who to watch out for; your brothers live so far away, you could say we're your only family. Roadblock, Francelia warned. Ugarte closed his eyes, may it be as God wishes, some people are always playing their last card.

They went through two military roadblocks and another put up by the Federal Police without any problem. Excuse me, are there a lot of checkpoints ahead of us? Señorita, I am not authorised to give you that information. Thank you, the good thing is that it doesn't make you any less handsome, and the uniform looks terrific on you. Maybe five from here to Sinaloa.

María took out her cell and reported that there were six calls from General Alvarado, the first at ten the previous night, the last at six in the morning; she read a message from her closest friend: Wake up honey, remember our date is at ten. Ugarte concentrated: the General is worried and for sure he suspects I'm headed for Culiacán to die where I was born. He thought about what answer to give his daughter. What if the General is having problems? If they're pursuing me so doggedly something extraordinary must be going on, who am I to deserve such attention? The Secretary already told me I don't exist. Will I be able to celebrate my sixtieth? not in Cuernavaca, it's off limits now, though it could be in Culiacán, people are always partying there, I could even invite Turk Estrada. But if the General is in trouble this thing must be coming to a head, he's the President's man; are they testing out

187

the elite group on us? what motherfuckers. As Pérez-Reverte would say, they won't take me alive.

Cold. Light mist. Highway packed with speeding vehicles. On the radio: Jesse & Joy's "Outer Space".

Thirty-Seven

What's with you, Mendieta, are you bent on turning everything to shit? just now Attorney Blake Hernández called again and he was furious; he demanded immediate action on his report about his brother, and what's more he told me the guy was attacked a second time at his business, which Hortigosa confirmed; fucking mother, what's wrong with you? Nothing, chief, Toledo went there to ask him where he was the night Dr Manzo got killed; since he wouldn't tell us when he was here, we made a house call. You still suspect him? Not really, it's just that we should complete the investigation and that piece of information is missing. Did you get it? No, the jerk is a spoiled brat and on top of it he's really dangerous, he was a champion in the kind of boxing where anything goes and he hasn't a shred of respect for the police; he told Zelda that if we brought a warrant from a judge maybe he'd tell us, but he warned her it won't be what she expects to hear. So forget about him, the brother is a thorn up my ass and I'd just as soon not know he exists. Careful, that commission has clout, I heard they defended some conscripts who raped a little old woman over seventy. If you stop bothering the engineer, for sure he'll forget about us. Send him a Christmas present. Don't make a joke of it, Lefty, you are part of why I'm fed up. Before anything else happens, let me report that we're on the case of a dentist murdered in Navolato, we've got the name of the criminal and . . . So what are you waiting for?

you want me to take you by the hand? we have jurisdiction in the whole state. The problem is it's Tenia Solium. Holy Mary, Mother of God, so what does Pineda say? He wishes us a merry Christmas and a happy New Year, but he gave us information on the man. Briseño leaned back in his chair. At least you'll leave Señor Blake Hernández alone. Mendieta smiled. I'm glad that makes you happy, chief, I can see you won't miss me if I leave everyone in the world alone. Don't get melodramatic; listen, how's your son? He stood up. Huge, he just got his first tooth. He walked out.

Boss, what should we do? Make babies, we could sell them. Aha, you're still feeling good, aren't you? Well, Agent Toledo, let's take it easy. Will you listen to that, I never expected that from you. Christmas is almost here, time to give presents and put on a few kilos, relax, why should we be the exception? Should we forget about Tenia? And Blake and Manzo and Glasseater too. Now you really are inspired, what about Mariana Kelly? Hmm, that's also going nowhere. What about Gori? what do we do with Gori? Well, I'm going to thank him for his present, it's really touching. The poor guy shouldn't have to face Christmas like that, his self-esteem's below his ankles. Fucking Gori, who would have thought it. Have you seen him?

He opened the door. Hortigosa was sitting at his desk, arms crossed, scowling at his torture equipment on the wall. What's up, my man Gori, what's keeping you out of trouble? Just hanging around, Lefty my man, I'm O.K., and the fact is I've decided to resign. What's that about? About the end of dedicating my life to service, my friend. So a little breeze makes you seasick? And my joints ache. Aha. Silence. A dude who was state karate champion is coming by, boss. What do we want with a guy like that? we're badges, a different breed of shit. Well, that's what I think, but the dude is coming, like it or not, they sent me a notice, it's a recommendation from the attorney general's office. Alright, let's stop dancing around it like jerks: you're upset because that bastard beat the shit out of you, right? He beat you up too. Well, yeah, but the one in trouble is you, that faggot can suck my dick. Uh-huh, Lefty the tough guy. That faggot can suck my dick, and I'm going to show you, but first let's make one thing clear: when has a dude in your profession ever tried to do his work with his hands? Never that I know of. So why do you want to do that, fucking Gori? what, you think you're Superman? you are a strong fucking bastard, but you've got limits, it's like a baker trying to bake bread in his underarm; no shit fucking Gori, that's why instruments were invented. Another silence. Gori, who had looked crushed, raised his head and brightened a little. For real? do you think? Fuck my mother if I don't; Gori, there are diapers for adults, why? for the simple reason they're needed. Silence. You speak well, my man Lefty, but who's going to bring me that cocksucker? Who do you think, you bastard? That reminds me, the chief was asking questions. He told me about it, and he agrees you should do what you want. Really? Absolutely, that guy's had his boots licked too much, it's time he learned policemen deserve respect. No shit.

He punched a number into his cell. What's up, my man Devil? how's it going? On target, Lefty my buddy, as a matter of fact, I reported to Señor Garcés and he wants to know if you still need me, and Chopper too. That's why I'm calling you. He gave him Blake's address, warned him that he was dangerous and said he wanted him as soon as possible at the Conservatory, the place where everybody either sings or learns to sing better than if they studied opera with Enrique Patrón de Rueda. Here's a question for you, Devil: is Tenia Solium with you people? He was, my man, but with all the shit going down, which you know all about, the dude set out on his own, now he's freelancing and the fact is he's trouble, are you after him? He killed one dentist for sure and we suspect he killed another. He's uncontrollable, the bastard, he's got bad teeth and his breath stinks like hell; if you need us to take him down, just tell the boss, we could take advantage of the fact that right now you two are having a fling. What's that about, my friend Devil? don't exaggerate. What I mean is you're getting along.

Ninety minutes later Urquídez called. My man Lefty, the jerk didn't show up to work and his employees don't know when he will, we staked him out but it's not a good idea for us to hang around there, what do you think? Go back about six.

They did. After an hour, the parts store closed, and Blake was still not to be found. Devil called in. O.K. my friend, like they say in the classics, there are days when you lose and other days when you stop winning. It's a rare thing for a match to end in a tie; one question, Lefty, my man: do you know about the Chúntaros? Well, I've heard of them. They're Tenia's sworn enemies and they more or less get along with us, I'm just saying, in case it's of any use. Now you're talking, and hanging up your stocking.

Two hours later, Susana, Mendieta and Jason were having dinner at El Farallón, when in walked Constantino Blake Hernández and Lizzie Tamayo. Bodies relaxed, satisfied expressions, lips reddened. Lefty did not react when he spotted them, did not even lose the thread of his conversation with Jason: Think of the toughest cop you can imagine, a guy who has never read a single book, and that's what he gets me for Christmas That's so strange, he must think you come from another planet. Of course there are badges who read and live normally, but not many of us; it's a profession that takes over your life. I read *Love in the Time of Cholera* and I liked it, all those telegrams and waiting for an eternity. Knowing how to wait is a virtue; out of the corner of his eye Lefty watched the couple showing off, she her legs, he his unbelievable arrogance. Susana smiled, she felt good being with these two men who were so similar. She was drinking slowly and since Schwarzenegger had not returned she felt happy, though still a bit nervous about that former lover who was bold enough to follow her here. A girl I know recommended *Lust for Life* by Irving Stone, about Van Gogh, a genius who liked his corn chowder with a whole ear. She adored Jason, and this man who seemed too innocent to be a policeman made her feel motherly; but they had not pinned down anything about support for her son, so she decided to lay her cards on the table. Edgar, what do you think: Should Jason become a policeman or should he go to college for another profession? Mama, we can talk about that some other time. Excuse me for interrupting, but I'm worried about it; since you don't want to train or compete we won't get a scholarship, and we've got to do something so you can continue your education. I'll put up the money, Lefty said, very sure of himself. But you haven't even asked how much it'll cost, and don't think it's cheap. Hey, I won't allow you to discuss my future, not at this table anyway; remember, I've already decided, so save yourselves the worry. You are so stubborn, police work is incredibly dangerous and though I might have found your reasoning charming before, now I think you ought to listen to us. Edgar filled her glass with white wine, hurried his whisky and asked for another; he put his attention on three young señoras chatting at the next table: What are you saying, Sally? the one with the big eyes asked. Laura's right, we'll go to Vallarta. Ooooooh. Are you serious about becoming a policeman? You know I already told you, of course, and I could be as famous as Eliot Ness. But I don't like it, these are violent times, and a policeman is really exposed. Well, maybe no profession is secure anymore, right now we're investigating the cases of two murdered dentists and a graphic designer, plus the beating of an engineer. Enrique told us you were attacked twice. Haven't you burned yourself cooking? A big smile from Jason: Lots of times, once she got an electric shock that laid her out on the floor, do you remember, Ma? being a chef is no piece of cake either. Why did they beat up that engineer? He won't tell us, they caught him coming out of a restaurant and took him away, that's all we know; I'm going to the bathroom. Jason answered a text. The señoras next door were having a ball planning a trip where they would take along their children but not their husbands: Oooooh. From the bathroom he called Devil and Gori.

Minutes later, when they were getting into the Toyota, they saw a black Hummer pull up to the restaurant door blasting "No Hay Chapo Que No Sea Bravo" by Los Tucanes de Tijuana. What awful music, Susana complained, they ought to outlaw it. Lefty turned on the stereo and Juice Newton's "Angel of the Morning" came on. Jason texted his cousin again: *spra ksa*.

Their animated chatter did not dim during the ride to the Col Pop. Susana talked about how Culiacán used to be, when there was no Forum and not so many cars, when Sunday afternoons they would take an *obregonazo*, a long walk down Obregón Avenue to look at all the other people. Why hasn't Enrique come back in so many years? He's afraid he'll stay, he's really impulsive. He could at least visit you, he talks about you all the time and you can tell he's dying to see you. Is he undocumented? That I don't know, has he told you anything about that, Jason? He says he's getting his papers in order. This is where we used to go to Mass, Susana said jubilantly when they passed Santa Cruz church. Edgar too? Did you come here, Edgar? because I don't remember ever seeing you. Once in a while; the shadow of Bardominos the priest crossed his mind weakly, minimised, controlled; he also thought of Dr Parra, bearded fuck, he must be shitfaced at some congress of Polish gynaecologists. Lots of the guys went once in a while; my sister Aracely, who got mixed up with Domingo and then had Gustavo, the cousin Jason hangs around with, she never set foot in church, Mama went crazy insisting. You see, that's why you shouldn't insist with me, I'm a good boy and I got a great Christmas present for being drug-free. You're right about that, though you ought to stick with athletics, what present? Oh, I'll tell you later. Did you give it to him, Edgar? Eh? Cavalry charge, it was Max Garcés: Mexicali man arrives in two hours, where shall I put him? At Las Quintas, but I'll see him tomorrow at ten. Click.

When they reached Susana's house, Jason said goodbye; Gustavo was waiting for him leaning on the Jetta, they were going to pick up the girls. Once Lefty and Susana were alone, they found each other's hands.

On the stereo: "If You Leave Me Now" by Chicago.

Do you have dreams?

No, what about you?

I do, nearly every night; I'm always young in my dreams, with my sisters or my friends; last night, for the first time I dreamed I was my age, I was with my sister Angelina, do you remember her? she's the eldest, the one who moved to Tijuana.

El Toro Valenzuela's girlfriend?

They never got that far, they only went out once, long before he became a big star; well, I had a dream about her: we're in a city where the streets don't have sidewalks and the only cars are racing cars zooming by us; we nearly get run over several times, we yell for help but nobody comes. We run toward a house that turns out to be a wall of rats' eyes staring at us, furious as could be, like they're inside glass bubbles. We don't know what to do. We're crying and hugging and praying.

Until L.H. turns up.

Who?

L.H., a friend of mine, he lives in Tijuana and he's got the guts of a hero.

I thought it was a brand of insecticide; well, somehow we manage to get into a mansion, it's the statehouse, full of señores, legislators in black suits who won't stop arguing. They all talk but nobody listens. We're so scared. The whole group turns to us and starts chanting in unison: sex is life, sex is life. Angelina starts dancing, making sexy moves, and several of them rush forward to touch her; she lets them, it excites her, she gets kind of horny; one of them throws his arms around her and she screams, then I woke up.

I never imagined anybody dreaming about legislators.

It was terrifying, I'm paying my dues for some sin; so put my mind at ease: will you come someday to visit us in Los Angeles?

You'd have to talk it over with Enrique so he doesn't get jealous.

I'll settle that with a few tacos al vapor, I could poison him without him even noticing.

Who is the gringo?

A pain in the butt, you saw.

What does he do?

He's a Marine, and I never had, do not have and never will have anything to do with him: Jason hates him and the feeling is mutual.

Why did he come?

Because he's a maniac; I told him clear as could be that I would never be with anyone who does not love my son, and he refuses to get the message. Maybe now he finally has; he hasn't been back, and I hope he won't be.

Let me know if he does, I've still got a few centimetres without bruises.

My hero.

Does Angelina still live in Tijuana?

She lives in Fresno; the only one who lives on this side is Aracely, Gustavo's mother; Gustavo's nine months older than Jason.

The one who wants to kill himself.

He's nuts, my sister says he wants to get his father's attention; the father is Colonel Domingo Félix, who's been at the Ninth Military Base for years.

I thought they moved them around.

They do, except for him, he must have worked something out; as a matter of fact, your bruises are practically gone, that doctor is an expert.

He's always fucking.

Just like you.

What do you mean? don't make things up.

I'm not making it up, want to see?

I do.

Thirty-Eight

Citicinemas. Night. A black Hummer in the parking lot.

An old Nissan Sentra pulls into the empty space to its right, and a moment later Turk Estrada gets out. No cats no dogs no. He gets into the back seat of the Hummer.

O.K., let's get down to what we're here for, I don't have much fucking time.

From the passenger seat Tenia Solium turns and reaches out his right hand in greeting, which the Turk rejects.

I haven't come to socialise, Tenia, and since you didn't kill Mariana Kelly we want the money back.

Steely gaze. Same look as when he was summoned.

Turk, I'm worth fuck-all, I can't find a fuckin' dentist to pull this tooth.

He points to his head tied up with a dirty rag. Uncle Beto at the wheel.

That's your problem, we paid you for something you didn't do and we want the dough back, and I see you're driving a new car. So that's all, and let me tell you, the boss isn't happy about the dentists dying and the scare you gave the one in Bachigualato. Manzo was our dentist and we liked him. Don't think I'm going to forget I sent you to him when we had our first chat at the Paraíso.

I didn't know you were so sentimental.

I couldn't give a fuck what you know or don't know, just hurry up with the moolah because Señor Arredondo wants what's his.

I couldn't get her in Mazatlán because of the tooth, but she got good and fucked anyway; that's what counts, right? Besides, when we saw each other the second time you said Samantha would be there; Mariana wasn't a sure thing.

Don't try to confuse things, Tenia, she was there and you didn't take her down, and now we have the Pacific Cartel stepping on our heels and a fucking tough bastard of a badge: Lefty Mendieta.

In-fuckin'-credible, that faggot got away from me once, a fuck-load of years ago; let me be the one to take him down.

You still don't get it, Tenia Solium, we're not interested, all we want is our money back.

Uncle Beto lit a cigarette.

Turk, if they don't pull this mother it's going to carry me off to fuckin' hell; help me, take me to another dentist.

You're fucking dreaming, you've got twenty hours, tomorrow at eight I'll expect you at the Comercial Mexicana Campiña parking lot, next to Coppel.

The Turk gets out. Tenia opens his door.

Aren't you going to say goodbye?

And he peppers him with bullets.

Nobody tells me to hurry, you prick, and if your fuckin' boss is such a macho let him come himself.

The Hummer rolls unhurriedly out of the lot. The Turk lies spreadeagled next to the little Sentra. Movie-lovers come out of the last show, chatting.

Thirty-Nine

Devil Urquídez and Chopper Tarriba entered the restaurant swaggering like cowboys.

They were wearing black leather jackets and baseball caps with the logo of the Culiacán Tomateros. Is someone expecting you? smiled the knockout of a hostess. We're guests of Señor Blake Hernández, could you point us to his table? The girl checked her list: Table forty-six, this way, please; he's with the blonde señora at the back. That's my aunt, thank you.

"White Christmas" by the Sinaloa Youth Symphony Orchestra, under the baton of Baltasar Hernández, on the sound system.

Señor Blake Hernández, come with us. The man scrutinised the recent arrivals warily. Who needs me? Lizzie glanced at the two gunslingers and sipped her cocktail, unconcerned. The top dog. Blake's expression was sour; they smiled, relaxed. Could you hang on for a few minutes? We don't mind, but the big man is in a hurry. That's what he said, added Chopper, who had blue eyes. Blake turned to the girl: If I'm not back in fifteen minutes, take a taxi. You are horrible, she threw her cocktail in his face, I hate you, then a plate with the remains of an aguachile at his chest. Hey, take it easy, don't start in with your fucking act, you're a big girl now. You are such a jerk, you boor, you lout. Lizzie was one of those women whose beauty shone when she got angry, she knew that of course.

Stepping out the door Devil gave him a wallop on the back that shook him to the core. Constantino tried to respond but Chopper put a gun to his head. Don't give us any trouble, you fucking fag-got, unless you want to be worth shit. Hey, take it easy, I get it, and just to say something he added, I know one of the heavies. Here the only heavyweights are us, asshole, another wallop. And shut your trap. Before putting him in the Hummer they frisked him, handcuffed him and put a hood over his head. Behind the glass door with the restaurant's logo the hostess was going over her reservation list and did not see a thing. Are you sure I'm the one you're looking for? What, you think we're blind? Devil cleared his mind with another blow, this time with his pistol. Hunk Gómez is my friend, from the Pacific Cartel, when he was young he worked with us at Blake's Auto Parts, I don't see any point in handcuffing and hooding me. You can explain that to the boss. Chopper pulled out. In the back seat Blake's anger quickly turned to fear. Do you know what they want me for? No-one answered; he tried to calm himself. The night of the murder of Dr Humberto Manzo Solís he had gone to see Gómez, who controlled a portion of the border between Mexicali and Tijuana. After waiting five hours in a house in the neighbourhood of Chapule, he got the interview and asked for a loan; it wasn't that much, he wanted to pay his workers their Christmas bonus and have something for the January drought. For sure now they had the money for him; so he stopped worrying and brought Lizzie's body to mind: Fucking witch, how does she manage to keep herself looking so good? it must be all that sex, does she ever love to spread her legs. Chopper turned down the volume on the stereo, "Lamberto Quintero" by Chalino Sánchez. That woman is addicted to sex, I can't help it that she's a widow, and what with Peraza off on vacation with his family, that must be why she flew off the handle, she wanted to do it again after supper; once I collect the money from the Hunk I think I'll drop in on her, I like driving her out of her mind, it's what the bitch loves.

They turned into the S.M.P. parking lot and pulled up at Gori's door, which Devil still recalled from his days as a badge. We're here, asshole. Would you take this mother off me? The señor will do it. Let's go, said Chopper, who had not opened his mouth during the ride, and he hauled him by the arm. Blake felt his strength. When they crossed the threshold, Blake noticed the acrid odour of the place, and as soon as they took off his hood he knew where he was. Devil put a gun to his forehead, Chopper put his to the back of his neck. One move and you've fucked your mother, you fucking pansy. Blake thought about it and continued walking, he spotted Gori and smiled, but not for long, Robles threw a bucket of cold water on him, and Gori connected an electrode to one leg, he tried to kick, but . . . Hey, none of that, cocksucker. Even with all this you can barely manage, eh gorilla, you're like every other badge, mediocre to the core. Robles swung a baseball bat and caught him on the back, he stumbled. You're a faggot, his voice shaking. Gori closed the circuit and gave him 220 volts. The engineer doubled over. Gori waved a thank you to Devil and Chopper, who departed satisfied. Let's see, Papa, so you're a real macho? he hit him in the crotch with the baseball bat. I hope you've already got kids, asshole. Uggh. Because if you don't, you never fucking will, where did you get the idea of messing with my old lady? you think you're hot shit, don't you? well, you are about to get royally fucked. He poured chilli powder into a bottle of Tehuacán soda water. We've got a camera here so you can send lots of pictures to your little brother, you fucking faggot, only these are going to be real.

If Blake and Gori ever discussed their perceptions of these Solaris-like moments, they would never agree, or would they?

Forty

Francelia was driving; she was listening to "Me Voy" by Julieta Venegas, the Tijuana crooner, and singing along: "*qué lástima pero adiós*". Her mother asleep, her father hanging on. They managed to get through Tepic without incident and Ugarte figured they could stop for a few days in Mazatlán, maybe at the Estrella Reluciente, which was on the outskirts, the people there were discreet and the women could relax at the beach if the weather was good. The unmistakable shadow was there in the corner of his eye, but that no longer tormented him, some adversaries simply cannot be beat. One hundred and twenty kilometres per hour. Francelia spied a checkpoint and slowed down. What is it? A checkpoint, Pa. The army? Looks like the Federal Police. They've got black uniforms, María added, more or less awake. The two old cars advancing slowly ahead of them were waved on, but not them; they were sent to a rest area next to where the roadblock had been set up. The one car behind them was waved on through. Where are you coming from? From Guadalajara and we're headed for Mazatlán. Fuck Mazatlán, you people are staying right here, get out and don't touch a thing, leave your bags, cell phones, money, everything you've got. But. Please, my husband is very ill. Then he's going to be the first one out, and you better hurry, we don't have any fucking time, or the story ends here. Don't be inhuman, look how sick he is. Shut your trap, you fucking bitch, if you don't I'll fuck him to save him the suffering, he pointed an A.K.-47; and we'll give you and the babe a nice screw so you don't go around saying we didn't take you into account. Let's get out, Ugarte mumbled, pulling himself together, there were too many for his little pistol; don't argue. The women opened their doors, then Ugarte's, who slid over slowly, trembling, in pain. Move it, fucking cows. Will you allow me to take along my husband's pills? he needs them. You aren't going to take a motherfucking thing, if he's going to die, let him die already, he looks totally fucked. Ugarte squeezed his wife's arm so she would not insist. Five young guys collected the orange cones that marked the checkpoint, climbed into the van and took off the wrong way, against the traffic. As their car receded into the distance, they watched in silence, absorbing what had just occurred. Bastards, Francelia said, did you see, Mama? they looked to be about my age. Take it easy, at least they left us in one piece. Now what? Someone will come along who'll take us to the nearest town; if there aren't any taxis there, we'll pay someone to take us to Mazatlán. Ugarte sat on the ground, he looked defeated, offended, besieged, without the medicine soon the pain would be torture. Do you have any money? because I spent all of mine in Guadalajara. A hundred pesos, the rest is in my bag with the credit cards and everything else. No truck will take us for that; Pa, do you have any? Nothing. They took the cell phones too. So we'll have to show off our legs, Ma and me. Don't push it, Ugarte touched the small Smith & Wesson Classic in his jacket pocket and gave thanks they hadn't frisked him, but he did not mention it, María did not approve of certain military traditions.

After twenty minutes with their thumbs out, a Nissan Frontier from way back in the twentieth century stopped. Driving it was a young rancher who blatantly ogled Francelia. What are you doing here? We got robbed, they took everything, van, money, credit cards: everything. Those bastards have been fucking with us for a while and they can't seem to catch the creeps; if you like I can take you to La Concha, listen, your friend looks really out of it, was it the fright that got him? He's ill. Get in then, in La Concha we'll find someone to take you to Escuinapa if you want to see a doctor. Would you take us to Mazatlán? Hmm, I don't know, when we get to town you can talk to Elías, he's my compadre, but he's a real tough nut, and he's the only one who has a good car; get in, my friend, one of you women climb in back.

An hour and a half later they were going seventy kilometres an hour in a Volkswagen Beetle with the radio blasting rancheras. On the outskirts of Mazatlán someone lent them a telephone, Ugarte called the Turk. We buried him yesterday, his son said, they killed him, and we don't even feel up to reporting the crime. Are you the lawyer? You could say that. The Turk told me about you, he had a lot of faith in you, so take care of yourself. Were you a friend of his? We went to high school together; now you've got to look to the future and become a success, that bit about keeping the Culichis from having street parties would be really hard to pull off, but it sounds smart. He told you about my thesis? Proud as could be, but he was really worried. Yeah, he told me that too, and the fact is I'm going to think it over, could you tell me your name? Of course, Ugarte, and take care of yourself because life has a lot of good to it; he could not help but recall his friend's words; and to think you were sure you would go after me, I hope St Peter doesn't give you any trouble. Then in the Mazatlán phone book he looked up the coordinates of the friend he had seen two years before in Scotts-dale getting treatment for a simple skin cancer. He called him at his office: Señorita, tell Architect Miranda that it's Héctor Ugarte, a friend from high school. A minute later: What's up, fucking Ugarte, are you here? Nearby, and don't thank me yet, I'm calling to ask a favour, how's your skin doing? It's like I'm fifteen again, you bastard, thank God, what about you? No, I didn't beat it, so I'm getting ready for that trip they say is really short: it lasts less than a second. Well, I heard it was really long because you never come back, so what's up? We got robbed near La Concha and they took everything; a taxi is taking us to Mazatlán and I'll need to pay the driver; I'm with my wife and my daughter. They cleaned you out of money, credit cards, documents, car, all that? Everything, even my visas for Canada and the United States. Tell him to bring you to my office and we'll take care of whatever you need, he gave him the address. Thank you, my friend. Don't start fucking with me now, you were always a real faggot, but you weren't sentimental. Hearing his old nickname, Ugarte knew the door would be open.

On the radio: Approximately two hours ago, on a major highway in the North, a southbound Windstar van, white with Tlaxcala plates, was gunned down by a commando unit of men in grey, according to eyewitnesses. At the scene the bodies of several passengers have yet to be identified because they were burned from head to toe. Ugarte closed his eyes. What group was General Alvarado talking about? María and Francelia clung to each other. My God, what monster had they awakened? what could this gentle man have done to make them so angry? who were those men in grey? who were the men lying dead in their house? María put a hand on her husband's shoulder and gave it a soft squeeze. The driver, paying no heed, whistled along to the ranchera.

Forty-One

The following day Blake looked pale in the interrogation room. He walked with difficulty. He grimaced in pain when he sat down. Zelda, enjoying her Diet Coke, took his statement. He was a wreck, eyes red, arm hanging loose, trembling and evidently burning with rage. The detective, in all formality, asked: Where were you the night of the murder of Dr Humberto Manzo Solís? Blake hung his head, his mocking tone and his arrogance were both gone. I was with Antonio Gómez, I waited for him from seven until twelve, then he saw me and I spoke with him for five minutes; he had to go to Mazatlán, he didn't tell me what for; I went to ask him for a loan so I could pay my employees their full Christmas bonus; he worked for us seventeen years ago and he's been good to me; three times he's helped me out of a squeeze, and I've paid him back on time; he's a real stickler when it comes to money, maybe because he grew up poor. Your alibi is not easy to confirm, Señor Blake. I know, that's why I didn't want to tell you, who's going to go ask the Hunk if what I'm saying is true? Why did he keep you waiting so long? He was with some babes. Zelda took a sip of her Coke. Why did you send those photographs to your brother? To mess with you. Well, it sure gave him an opportunity to play the hero, he won't leave us alone. I know what Attorney Blake is like, he's been that way since he was a child. Are you going to send him something now? This is where it dies, sometimes you lose and other times you stop winning. What day did Gómez go to Mazatlán? After he spoke with me, he had an appointment, he didn't say what and that's got nothing to do with me. Precisely, how did you become so good at fighting? Oh, I trained in boxing and karate, is that a crime now? Pause while Zelda took another sip. You cannot leave the city. Am I still a suspect? Until I confirm your alibi, have you seen Lizzie Tamayo? Every day. Can I know why? Because our relationship is sexual, don't tell me you don't do it every day. Have you heard of Tenia Solium? Crime is not my specialty, señorita, and now that I've had a look, neither is it yours. What about Gómez, is he a sister of charity? The man pursed his lips. Merry Christmas, Señor Blake. Don't fuck with me with that, señorita.

Everything O.K., Zelda my girl? Gori was smiling happily. Perfect, my man Gori, and you, did you sleep through the night? Like a freshly castrated priest; listen, if you need me, just call, I'm going to find a present for my father-in-law and another for my goddaughter now that I know it isn't so hard. Gori, take your wife and your daughter along, we women love to go shopping, we even forget about life's troubles. They'll shop me out of house and home. It's Christmas, Gori my friend, you should do everything as a family, this afternoon Rodo and I are taking my mother shopping. Then I'll do as you say, what about Lefty? He'll be here soon, he's out buying presents with his son. Yikes, everybody's doing that, maybe I'll run into him; by the way, he thanked me for the book. You impressed him. That's what he said, so I'll see you later, Zelda, and thank you, I owe you one.

*

Lefty entered the cartel's safe-house in Las Quintas at 11.30 in the morning. Max Garcés and Hyena Wong were waiting for him. They were smoking, joking, evoking past adventures. The Hyena had snorted enough to keep him from getting anxious. Garcés introduced them. Wong was a little older than Mendieta, shorter and thinner. I was telling Max that I know something about you, copper, something about back when we were little squirts. Lefty studied him: yellowish skin, bony, pronounced Asian features, neat black moustache. Don't remind me of the good old days, Wong, the farther away they get, the happier I am. The Hyena smiled, nodding. Then I'll only say once upon a time we called you the Cat, because you had nine lives, you must remember. The past will set us free, Lefty lit a cigarette, refused to dredge up memories, gave it a puff and spoke up. You said on the telephone that you attended a meeting in Mazatlán representing your cousin Wang. Yeah. That you seemed to recognise the guy from Hermosillo from someplace else. I couldn't be dead sure, but that dude, I know I set my eyeballs on him before in some other busyness; on the plane I was racking the noodle and it won't quite fill in the blank, but I'll be damned if I can place the others either, there were three or four buddies I'd never seen. Max perked up. But that dude from Hermosillo, it was just the way I remembered you, his face in my mind, but I can't be sure. Make an effort, do you think he was on your side or the other? The feeling I get, like he was the law, but I can't say for dead certain, you know what a bitch Ah-old-timer's is; I couldn't believe how pale he was, like he was nervous, you could tell when the señora asked how things were in the territories; he said fine, his voice was firm; but that needle's pricking at my brain even more now with what happened. You remember him from before. Yeah, maybe years ago, like you. Mendieta turned to Garcés, who gave him a subtle signal that they could talk afterward. In this business you get all kinds, Mendieta. Don't I know it, Devil is a good example, he looked at the Hyena, whose eyes were black, small, lethal; he had heard a lot about his cruelty and his effectiveness, of his cousin Wang's rise to success with him as his lieutenant. Did you notice anything strange in any of the three or four you mentioned? Nope, but I didn't know them, all the rest I'd set eyes on at least once, the guys from Tijuana I know I know, I'm one of the few who've been in the organisation forever, the San Luis people too, and the dudes from Juárez. Do you remember what time the meeting was? About eight-thirty. Did the one from Hermosillo arrive before or after you? Before; a serious dude, maybe too serious, he sat right beside me at a long, long table. What were his hands like? What's this about, copper? well, maybe if the dude had been a babe, but I'm no faggot, no, I've got nothing to say. I want to know if they were strong. Now that you mention it, they were normal, they didn't seem weak. Max told me he was wearing a leather jacket. It was a little big for him. On his body? On his arms too, you could say the dude wasn't exactly ripped. O.K., like I said, we're looking for Mariana Kelly's murderer and anything could be helpful. My cousin Wang is really hurting, he even closed his restaurant for a day in mourning; Max, if I can't see La Jefa, tell her my cousin hopes her sorrow will soon pass. I'll tell her. Copper, I'm so glad you left Narcotics, you know back then we weren't so quick to get back at people, because now you step out your door and you don't know if you'll ever come back. Regular people say the same thing; let's see, Wong, you've been around the longest, do you think one of the guys at the meeting was involved in killing Mariana? No matter who I knew or didn't know, I'm saying they hired a professional; I'm not accusing anyone, but I've seen things, and the truth is I wouldn't put my hands into the fire for any of them. Especially the ones you don't know. To begin with, but even the ones I know I know. What do you mean? interrupted Max Garcés, stubbing out his cigarette on the floor. Well, just that, after what happened with Eloy Quintana, that bastard had been with us from the very beginning, and despite the fact we took him and his people down, there'll always be somebody who might get the notion of hitting where it hurts most. I hear you, we think the assassin got in by the window after rappelling down from the roof. Really? well, then you'd have to cross off half of them, copper, they're obeast and we were all pretty juiced; before the meeting, which was delayed a bit, we guzzled two bottles of whisky with those little drops you must know all about, we were in my room, everybody except for the dudes I didn't know. What about the one from Hermosillo? He stopped by, stayed a while, he had a drink and disappeared without saying goodbye; but that's normal, the bros never say goodbye: it's bad luck. Right. I wasn't paying much attention then, but I eyeballed the whole bunch and he was one of them; at the meeting I got a better look-see. None of the others seemed nervous to you? They looked normal, listening closely to La Jefa, reporting on their shit. Did you head off to continue drinking once the meeting was over? Continue drinking? no way, we were out of there like bullets, that's what you always do. So you didn't see the guy from Hermosillo again? No, the only one I saw was the buddy from San Luis who went back with me in my cousin's plane; several of the bros had their planes at the airport: it's the best way to get home in a hurry, but I didn't see him; now that we're finishing up, I'm out of here, there's a party tonight and I don't want to miss it. O.K., as soon as you remember where you saw the Hermosillo guy before, you let me know, and if something turns up we'll give you a call. The Cat we used to call you, copper; the bros who did the car trick on you never imagined you were going to get out alive. Leave their names with Max, just in case. No point: except for one, they're all dead. So, divine justice. They smiled.

Devil and Chopper came to take the Hyena to the airport.

Max told him: Wong doesn't trust Durazo, our representative in Hermosillo, he says he was a good friend of Eloy's, but Quintana was everybody's friend; and the ones he didn't know are the gringos, all trusted by their bosses. Could the bit about the leather jacket tell us something? Half of them were wearing leather jackets. In other words, we're fucked. And full of holes in the middle. I'm looking for a rock-climber, the Hyena said half of them were obese, did you see anyone skinny enough to rappel down easily? Several of them, but that isn't much to go on. What time is the guy from Hermosillo coming? At three o'clock, and you know what? he's not exactly a piece of spaghetti. No? He must weigh ninety kilos and he's uncoordinated as hell. Well, when you've got him here, let me know.

Mendieta felt they had managed to get nowhere, it was a complicated case, particularly because of the people he would have to interrogate, why didn't Hyena Wong want to spill anything over the telephone? What he said wasn't any big deal, was he testing him, to see how tough he was? Fuck him, if he's hiding information the only thing he'll do is slow us down; and that bullshit of bringing up my past, was there something there? So they're all dead except for one, eh? I'm getting tired of these assholes. He figured if he wanted to get his adrenaline up and running he'd have to go after Tenia Solium, but as soon as they got to their feet, the din of a deadly gunfight reached them from the street. Max grabbed an A.K.-47 and ran out. Iraq. Intense fire. Afghanistan. Exploding bombs. Culiacán. Three men who had been standing guard were up on the high metal wall shooting like demons into the street. Lefty at his side, Max asked, What's up? Our guys are out there, somebody was waiting for them. Why haven't you used the bazooka? give it to me, he handed Lefty the A.K.-47 and picked up the bazooka. There's no angle to fire. Max climbed up and took a look, then stepped down and went over to Drysnot, who was shooting nonstop. Let me by, loco. He clambered up then dropped to his haunches because at that moment they came under sustained fire. Lefty's mouth fell open. Garcés leaped up and let loose a deafening blast from the bazooka. Vrooom. A dark hummer flew through the air and another put the pedal to the metal and vanished. Sepulchre. Max climbed down, and everyone went over to the dark-green iron gate. Lefty, as he later admitted, was prepared to shoot. The armoured S.U.V. had survived with about three hundred holes in the body and two flat tires. Devil put it in reverse and got it into the yard. Let's go; Mendieta, you head out first, Max ordered. No fucking way, I leave with you or I don't go. The men emptied out of the car: Devil and Chopper, adrenaline to the max, Hyena Wong unflappable, holding the burning hot A.K.-47 he had used to respond to the attack. They climbed into Max's armoured Tundra, Lefty got into his own Toyota, the rifle still in his hand, and the bodyguards piled into a black Hummer. Copper, my man, Wong shouted, I know who that dude is, when I get to Mexicali I'll give you a call. They sped off. Sure, you'll call whenever you fucking feel like it, he mused. The Toyota in the middle. The neighbourhood as if nothing had happened.

What is that bastard doing? It bothered Max that Mendieta was holding his position in the caravan. He's going to follow us, said Devil Urquídez at the wheel, until Señor Wong tells him what he has to tell him. Well, he's going to have to follow us all the way to the airport. He's a bastard, that badge, we used to call him the Cat.

Before Hyena Wong stepped into the zone for small aircraft, Lefty approached him. You are a tough one, copper, the real thing, and I'm glad you didn't die. Tell me about the dude. He was the law, I'm sure. Do you remember his name? What's with you, the rat-a-tat got the gourd to kick over but not that much; Max ought to know, at least the name he used at the meeting in Mazatlán; the name I do happen to recall is what they call the only dude still alive of the jokers that blew up your wheels and then sprayed you with bullets. They looked into each other's eyes. Valente Aguilar, better known as Tenia Solium. No shit.

*

We don't do it that often, could that bastard be screwing somebody else? if he is, I'll cut off the sonofabitch's balls; maybe we should do it more, it relaxes you, makes you happy and it brings you closer together, even the boss is going around like a leaf of lettuce; that would keep him satisfied too, I don't want some slut he might run across to turn his head. Ring. It was Robles: Agent Toledo, they called in a seven-four-six in Las Quintas. Got it. She called Mendieta: Boss, a gunfight in Las Quintas, should we go? Who called it in? A neighbour telephoned 086, it's near Estado de Puebla Street. I was there. What? It has to do with the Kelly case, that's the house I chose for interrogating suspects, somebody was out hunting and the bang-bang went on for a long while, there must be bodies because they blew up a Hummer. What do we do? Wait for me, I can't go in the Toyota. They already called the forensic doctor and two of Ortega's boys are on their way. We'll catch up to them, it happened about forty minutes ago, I'm pulling up to Headquarters right now.

Hummer roasted. Bodies burned to a crisp. Three A.K.-47s and four pistols all charred. The iron gate of the cartel's house showing smallpox. A couple of housewives peeking out their windows, a chubby man heading to the super. Lefty, do you have any idea what happened here? Fucking Quiroz, why didn't you stay in Colombia? Hey, I brought coffee for you, so you can learn what it really tastes like. You should have stayed, maybe by now you'd be the correspondent for *¡Hola!* or *Hello!*. Listen, what's your theory about this? Notwithstanding what the commander might say, I hear there's a P.C. safe-house nearby, it's probably that one that got all shot up, and people say a heavyweight from the North and another from around here were in there having a meeting, I even heard a detective on a case was present. Whoa, Lefty, what a lousy friend you are, what would you lose by telling me what you think or what you've heard? If you want I'll write your article for you, you fucking media slave. You only talk nonsense, how can I do journalism right if you won't talk to me? Don't lose your temper, Pineda's sure to be here soon, he's the one who knows all the dope on this. I thought you were my friend. Don't be a crybaby, fucking Quiroz, did the Colombians treat you so badly? And here I was thinking I might get fresh information from you. You also believe in God and you never curse; wait for the anti-drug tsar and stop flapping your gums, he won't be long.

In an hour all that was left of the confrontation was a stain on the road. They were returning to Headquarters when Zelda Toledo's cell phone rang. Hello. Señorita, I hope you haven't forgotten me. Who's speaking? Glasseater, the performer with an exclusive engagement at El Quijote. I can hear you fine, Rodelo, I'll put the boss on; Lefty continued: What's up? did you polish off all the bottles in La Pipima? Worse, I had to flee; a buddy there, Nacho Trejo, warned me that Tenia's people were looking for me; I'm here with the whole family. Seriously? Fear doesn't travel by burro. O.K., go to the Hotel El Mayo and get a room, we'll call now to let them know. What about El Quijote? We'll see about that tomorrow.

Zelda made the calls. Lefty told her about his conversation with Hyena Wong and said they ought to announce José Rodelo's debut for the next day. Did you speak with the owners? No, but I bet

219

Tenia likes the show. As long as we're bringing each other up to speed, three days ago an older man was killed in the Citicinemas parking lot, but the family wants to let things lie, his name was Samuel Estrada. Samuel Estrada? that sounds familiar. It should, he's on the list of Dr Manzo's patients. I suppose, anything else? He's got a record: he did time in La Mesa for drug trafficking, stockpiling weapons issued exclusively to the army and resisting authority: nearly twenty years in the shadows, he got out two years ago. Hmm, of course; Agent Toledo, you are a first-class Toledo; it's time you took your first graduate course, we'll set that up soon. There's more, I spoke with the son. With Jason? Zelda smiled. No, with Estrada's son, a smart kid, he told me his father had a slip of paper with a name in the pocket of the jacket he wore every day, "Antonio the Hunk Gómez, Maz", and that he did errands for Carlos Arredondo. Another of Manzo's patients and a very active narco, according to Terminator. Gómez is a friend of Blake's and he told him he was headed to Mazatlán without saying what for. Alright, let me take that up with Max. The point is that Arredondo called the son, promised to help the family out and named the culprit, can you guess who? Tenia Solium.

No shit.

Forty-Two

In three hours Ugarte's friend, an architect with connections all over, had them set up with a place to stay, passports and enough money to get by for a few days. Thankful, they avoided making any calls from his telephones, a detail the architect did not notice. All he thought was: Everybody makes a mess with his own shit. What he could not fail to note was that the dynamic but clingy boy from high school had disappeared, and in his place was a wretched bag of bones. The poor bastard, he was a good egg. María convinced him to get her a bank account where she could deposit his generous loan; then she called her friend Loretta from a public telephone and asked her to send enough money with someone she trusted. María, I'm totally freaked out, this morning I went by your house and a bunch of men in grey suits were lined up outside, guarding it, what happened? are you alright? Something spectacular happened, I'll tell you about it later. Just give me an idea, my husband was with me and he said by the look of those guys it must be something heavy; I went back a little while ago and everything looked normal, as if you were still there, I even felt like knocking. It isn't easy to explain, for the moment don't go anywhere near the house and don't telephone me either, right now I'm calling from a pay phone; I'll give you the details when I can, for now be happy that we're alive and safe, and please do me that great favour I asked.

At dusk, at the fishermen's monument people call Brutes in the

Buff, someone would hand her a lime-green suitcase with plenty of cash.

Moni will lend me money, she told Ugarte, caressing his hair, now completely grey and somewhat longer than official regulations would permit. I'll use it to buy more medicine and pay back your friend, the light-brown skin of her angular face looked soft. For the past eight years she had been in a relationship with Loretta Livingston, the woman who had just proved she would stand by her. The husband, a wealthy importer–exporter of fragrances, had agreed without comment. How will she get it to you? She explained. As you can see, I learned a few tricks from you. I'll go. You, why? you're really fragile, don't push yourself. Is Fran-celia in the swimming pool? No way, she's in the surf, riding the waves and chugging salt water like crazy; you know she's as reck-less as you are. They were at the Hotel Playa, resting in a spacious room facing the sea. There is something I've got to tell you, María. Another secret? there's no denying it, you like to dole out the details of your life with an eye-dropper; but there's no need to, Héctor, we've lived the way we've lived and that's how it turned out for us; dear woman with a penis, you don't have to make eleventh-hour confessions. It's important. What, that you slept with most of my friends, including Loretta? they already told me; so, better you should rest. Silence broken only by the sea. I killed Mariana Kelly.

María Leyva's expression went from astonishment to rage as she pulled away from her husband; if there was anything at all she knew about him, it was that he was lethal. You are a son of a bitch. Ugarte felt lucid, powerful, in charge; he felt his blood flowing, even the pain eased off for a moment, an extraordinarily critical moment in which he had his wife's entire attention. María got to her feet disgusted, took a step back to keep from strangling the vermin with her bare hands, how could he have possibly done something so abominable? Yes, I put a bullet between her eyes, Ugarte said with a vindictive sneer; María resisted the urge to suffocate him, skin him alive, burn him to a crisp. As soon as she recognised me, I told her she owed me a debt, that she was going to die for what she did to me; I had sworn as much eighteen years before and she remembered. It wasn't her fault, she'd been with Samantha since we were teenagers; if anyone was a culprit it was me, since I was always after her; then I consoled myself with an appalling sexual aberration, you. She didn't take it badly; she was coming out of the shower, didn't resist when I led her to the bed, she sat down and I shot her in the forehead with the Smith & Wesson, then I collected the shell and the cartridge. All vengeance is absurd, but vengeance for love is just plain stupid; after so many years, woman with a penis, how could you dare? The heart never forgets, María, and mine is a computer chip. And of course, all this lunacy you've dragged us into has to do with that, they must be looking for you all over the world. I went to a meeting with Samantha afterwards, I felt like rubbing her face in it, but I wanted to spend my final days with you; I gave her a bit of an insolent look to let her know the damage I had done her, she felt something because she shook my hand vigorously and frisked me with her witch's eyes. María stormed out on to the balcony, anger consuming her; evidently the next step was up to her. Ugarte turned on the television.

Javier Solórzano was reading out the news of the death of General Atenor Alvarado in the sun-bleached city of Mérida. Shot down at seven a.m. while jogging along Paseo Montejo; a man close to the President, who this morning lamented the death of an exemplary Mexican, that is how the President put it, and announced the creation of a special corps to put an end to organised crime. Who did we interfere with, General? Who is making us pay so dearly? Not the Secretary, he's an imbecile, and if it isn't him, then who? My God, the President? Alvarado was his top envoy for dealing with the drug gangs, the only one of his advisers who suggested negotiating peace at any price. Those were his plans and his desires, and I ruined them. Is it the war they want to put an end to? Or is it the Pacific Cartel? Of course, the Mochis Initiative, and we were in the way; what can you say, the General owed me a few.

He felt satisfied after so many years of waiting and wanting, but never had he imagined he would experience such peace; he felt the weight of his pistol lying on his abdomen and concluded there was no reason to put it off, what for? One of his objectives, perhaps the most important, had been achieved flawlessly. Through the window he saw the silhouette of a mermaid and the fatal shadow fluttering in the corner of his eye.

He turned the television off.

Forty-Three

At a house the cartel kept near the airport, Lefty met up with Nicanor Durazo. The man was heavyset and very sweaty. Have you got relatives in Sinaloa? My mother's from here, one of her sisters works in the government, I don't know exactly what she does but she's some big caca; when I was a kid we always spent our vacations here. Tell me about the meeting in Mazatlán. Durazo glanced at Garcés, who indicated he could go ahead. It was short, we were eight plus the señora, since I got a room on the first floor I was the last one there, about eight o'clock; I was worried because a long time went by before the Bogeyman came to tell me she was ready for the meeting, the way we'd agreed. What did you do in the meantime? They were showing "The Man with the Golden Arm", dubbed into Spanish, I really like Frank Sinatra, so I was glued to the tube. How long have you been doing rock-climbing? Me? crazy is one thing I'm not, the only sport I do is the open bar. You went to Wong's room before the meeting. But I didn't stay; besides not being one of the saints he prays to, there was nowhere to sit. I didn't know there was trouble between you two, Max interjected. It was about a woman, that happens sometimes; I didn't know he was looking to be her guy until he gave me shit. I hope it doesn't get out of hand. For me it's water under the bridge, did you interrogate Wong? He's one of the last, Mendieta said and decided to stop there, the only thing this guy has in common with

Tarzan is the moustache, in other words, nothing. Did you see anyone acting strange: nervous or excited? No, nor was there much light to see by, the only thing I remember is the smell: freshly cut roses.

In a few minutes he was alone with Garcés. They lit cigarettes. That bastard couldn't rappel if he was hanging from my balls, besides he was the last to show up and the Hyena said the guy he fingered arrived before him; Max, we're missing somebody, if the security, Drysnot aside, worked to keep outsiders out and it wasn't a professional hit man, then it was someone who was both things: a professional and a lieutenant; I'd like to speak with Samantha, how is she doing? Down in the dumps, sheesh, do dames ever love each other to death. They are really something, you're right; Max, where were you when Mariana Kelly got murdered? In the meeting room greeting the guests. Who accompanied Samantha to the meeting room? The Bogeyman and two more. They smoked. Did you know Samuel Estrada? The Turk, of course, what about him? He's dead, Tenia Solium killed him. Max dragged hard on his cigarette. Back in the beginning, when Don Marcelo was still alive, the Turk was one of ours; he got picked up the same night they killed my father, may he rest in peace, and he did twenty years; ever since he got out he's been with Arredondo, who by the way is on the rise, and if we don't keep an eye on him, in a few years he'll be pushing us aside; the Turk hated the Valdés family, he thought we'd set him up. So he must have sung like a canary in prison. Fact is, he didn't, it turns out what he wanted was to take revenge himself, he was fierce, really bitter; besides, when you're in the can and you drop a name you're fucked, you've got to give them all up. Why would Tenia kill him? That guy would kill his own mother, that's why we don't want him.

The afternoon was not too hot, they were sitting in rocking chairs by a window with the Japanese blind pulled shut. Max offered him a snort, Lefty took a small grain and put it on his tongue, left it there for a few seconds, then spit it out. I don't want you to get me hooked, the cure will be worse than the disease. Garcés put a respectable dose up his nose. Listen, what's the story on Hunk Gómez? Strange you should ask: yesterday he called and requested permission to take you down. Oh, yeah? He won't touch you, not even with a rose petal, do you know why he wanted to kill you? You tell me. You tortured one of his friends. Ah, the bastard Diablo and Chopper grabbed at El Farallón. And there's something there: the Hunk was supposed to be at the meeting in Mazatlán, but he slept through it; even so, somebody from Tijuana showed up, and we haven't figured out who he was, not even they know. Mendieta shifted in his seat. Why didn't you tell me this before? you greeted them all. Max smoked. As you know, it was a meeting of lieutenants so it's no surprise to see people we've never met, it's one way the kingpins protect themselves; the Hunk went to Mazatlán, but he partied with some babes, he didn't admit he was the one they sent until yesterday. Could he be the murderer? Hmm, I don't think so, he's even clumsier than Durazo. Somebody took his place, that's the bastard we haven't pinned down. And it's very likely he's the buddy the Hyena is fingering, remember he was half drunk and, as you might have noticed, he's pretty spaced, he

227

could have mixed up who was from where. I want to speak with the Hunk, they found a scrap of paper with his name on it in Turk Estrada's clothing, just maybe he had some contact with the interloper. That won't be possible, didn't I tell you he wouldn't touch you even with a rose petal? this morning we put thirty bullets in him. Then I guess not. The detective reflected: With the Turk dead too that line of investigation is going nowhere fast.

I remember a shrimpy guy wearing a leather jacket, a bit haggard, about seventy or seventy-five years old; I only saw him for a moment; the Hunk didn't know what to say when I asked who had come in his place. Maybe Samantha got a better look at him, call her.

The boss of the Pacific Cartel brightened when Max told her there might have been an infiltrator in Mazatlán. He handed the telephone to Lefty. Samantha Valdés, do you remember the guy from Tijuana? He was very handsome, I even told him so, good-looking despite his age; I was going to call his boss to ask about him because we were expecting Hunk Gómez, but with all this mess it went right out of my head. Tall? About five foot six, more or less, like me, thin, straight as an arrow, and he had a peculiar smile when I shook his hand, which by the way was soft, a bit effeminate, but strong; was he the bastard? That I don't know yet, I'll keep you posted, but he's a good place to start; did he remind you of anything or anyone? maybe you knew him. Nothing struck me, but you know how these things are; listen, if it's him you've got to find him. I know, but he's turned to smoke. If you need resources, just ask Max. Before you hang up: what was his peculiar smile like? She fell silent. I don't know, like he felt superior, he was a handsome man, the kind any woman would want, sort of like Leonardo DiCaprio or Brad Pitt. But those guys are uglier than punching God on Good Friday. Lucky you that you can kid around, Lefty Mendieta. Sorry, thank you, we'll be in touch. The detective hung up abruptly because his cell had gone crazy. It was Susana. He listened. Daylight no longer filtered through the Japanese blind. Max, I have to take care of a personal matter, call Wong before he goes to his family party, maybe he's remembered the name of the guy who gave him a bad feeling; it's obviously not Durazo.

He found a very upset Susana at home with Jason. A gringo, who identified himself as Jackie Chan, had turned up asking for Arnold Schwarzenegger, Jason said. He could have been a dead ringer for him if he weren't short and slight and Asian.

Do you remember me? To be frank, no.

I went to your restaurant once, with a friend who was looking to go out with you, a big strong guy. Oh, you did, did you?

I'm looking for him, have you seen him? He's at the Hotel Tres Ríos and we haven't seen him for four days; maybe he went back to Los Angeles.

He didn't; he's got an implanted chip that went down a few days ago. Is that so?

It does that when the person travels to the moon or gets buried. What! you mean he died?

I don't know, we talked every day, always about you; I'm betting he wouldn't have dug into his arm to remove the chip and bury it.

I hope he's alright; he came here several times to ask me out to lunch or supper, but I wouldn't go.

He was really in love with you. More like infatuated, I'd say.

That boyfriend of yours, the one he fought with, where can I find him? He's a detective, I suppose at Police Headquarters.

His name? Edgar Mendieta.

He said he was going to look for you and all he wanted was to find his friend, dead or alive. Susana looked pale, alarmed, worn down. Is there something you haven't told me, Edgar? About that guy, nothing, as you can imagine he's not somebody I lie awake at night thinking about. Mama, you shouldn't have given him his name, Marines are really tenacious when it's a question of one of their own. It's alright, Jason, nothing's going to happen, there's nothing to hide; I'm sorry if I blew it. Don't get upset, for sure tomorrow he'll turn up at Headquarters and I'll clear up what I can for him; from what you've told me, I'm guessing he got killed. That's what he led me to understand. So, we're up against the Marines, said Jason, isn't that something; I've heard with those chips they can locate you anywhere in the world. Call the Tres Ríos and ask for him. Jason looked at him anxiously, then smiled and went to find a telephone book.

He hasn't been back in four days, the young receptionist said, intrigued. O.K., I'll wait for the Marine to come to Headquarters, if he's investigating the case and isn't from Interpol, we can't offer much help, but don't worry, the gringos rarely need our assistance on cases like this; I bet the big oaf is drinking himself silly in Altata, would you like to go out for something? You two go, Gustavo and

I have a date with the girls. Does he still want to kill himself? Not anymore, now he's joined the club and he wants to be an officer like his dad. But he hated that, how did you convince him? He did it all by himself, the colonel came over to give him some money for Christmas and they spent a long time talking, he's really pleased to have his son follow in his footsteps. I want you to follow your own. Please, Mama, take it easy, go out and have a good time, and don't be home late, you'll keep Grandma up and she'll be haunting the house like a ghost. Lefty answered a call from Zelda. Boss, don't look for me at Headquarters. I won't. I left a while ago, after talking with Lizzie Tamayo, who came in with her sword drawn for what we did to Blake Hernández. Seriously? She said she never lodged a complaint against anyone, certainly not against him, and she doesn't want to know who murdered her husband, as far as she's concerned we can forget all about it. We'll take her suggestion into account. Ortega called to say there are no prints on the rappelling equipment and he has nothing more to report; about the videos, they're damaged, boss, all you can see are black lines, I don't think they'll be any help at all. Alright, take it easy.

In the Toyota he turned on the stereo: "Bette Davis Eyes" by Kim Carnes.

They went to El Quijote, which was packed.

Curlygirl's eyes grew wide when he recognised Susana Luján. Honeychild, this is outrageous, you look exactly the same, gorgeous as ever and still with your perfect derrière. You're the one who looks great, Curlygirl. They hugged. Lefty, I'm so glad you brought her, we'll get your table ready right away.

Susana cut a swath, the drinkers took one look at her body and comments began to flow; Mendieta liked that, he could count on the fingers of one hand the times he had been out with a beautiful woman admired by all, especially in a happening place like El Quijote. The vocalist of the norteño group was chiding the crowd: Of course, for sure, we'll play all the corridos you want, but first, sticking out his belly, caress what's hanging from me, you bastards. Fuck your mother, people yelled. Your dear mother can do it too, we don't want anybody to feel left out. Coolchicks, tell the one about the G.M.O. chilli. Sit down and I'll tell you, Papa. You're a faggot. That's what you used to think, tell the bros how you felt after I was done with you, don't be shy, Pissass, that's just the way you were born. Sing already, asshole, you're like an old woman who won't shut up. Did you hear that? that was my wife, her word is law; my dear, what are you doing here? you've got my whole pay-cheque already, you say it's not enough? not enough for the pot on the stove or for the flame in your belly? yes, sure, yes, of course, of course; "La Banda del Carro Rojo", a hit from the immortal Tigres del Norte! let's hear it for the little town of Rosa Morada, you faggots; and fuck the mother of whoever turns tail. Come on, sing already, Coolchicks, and stop talking bullshit.

They were seated in a secluded spot and were served roast beef tacos, beer and salsa mexicana. Paper wraps stone, Lefty said, smiling, then without knowing why, he told Curlygirl about Jason. Aha, so you two had something going, eh? congratulations; but listen, I won't ever tire of telling you how great you look, you've got to give me the recipe. But you don't look so bad yourself, Curlygirl, you've still got that soft skin and creamy complexion, which is the hardest thing of all to keep. I have my secrets too, we should trade, don't you think? what a surprise, Lefty, what a surprise. Stop making such a fuss and bring us more beer. Oh, come on, it's been years since I've seen this beauty and you don't want me to enjoy it? so how old is the kid? Eighteen. And just now trying out his dad, that's great. Curlygirl went off to his work, and the two of them looked at each other. His body had been asking for action for several minutes, but Lefty had kept it more or less under control. Susana took his hand and looked into his eyes. Would you really come to Los Angeles? Right away, as soon as you go, I already looked into it; it's a village near Guasave, right? Edgar, I can't believe what's happening, how well you and Jason are getting along, and, yes, us too after so many years. We're an urban myth. I love you, Edgar: earnest, unblinking gaze, holy hand; I'm serious. Curlygirl, who heard her words, discreetly placed the bottles of beer on the table and slipped away. The detective felt his entire being begin to vibrate, felt that God exists and lives nearby in the Col Pop. His body was humming happily and announced it with an explosive erection. Hey, take it easy, everything in due course. Your thing is sending me signals, Lefty, I swear. Hang on, don't get ahead of me. The Seventh Cavalry Charge interrupted. Mendieta here. I called the Hyena, the guy was from the military, he remembers him from twenty-odd years ago and his name is Edgar Iriarte. He's got my name? So it seems. Thank you, Max.

Lefty turned toward Susana, who was sensually applying burgundy red to her lips. She looked even more beautiful than every other time he had been with her. I love her too, he thought. I love her a fuck of a lot; and yes, I would like to live with her for the rest of my life; as the Beatles would say: here, there and everywhere; I'd have a ball with Jason. His body cried out, but in vain: he was feeling so romantic all he could think was: "I only believe in what I touch, and you, woman, I touch right to the core." Sincerely, Jaime Labastida.

They left the place hugging, kissing, and drove away listening to "Stumblin' In" by Suzi Quatro and Chris Norman. They failed to see the Asian shadow who made sure they did not slip from view. Neither did they see the other two shadows, who grabbed the first, hooded him, beat him, stuffed him in the trunk of a dark car and drove off along a familiar route.

Forty-Four

What did María tell her daughter about Ugarte? The truth; she told
her about his obsessive love for Mariana Kelly, how brutally he had
suffered from it eighteen years before and how she never thought it
would go so far. You were a baby. She paused and stared into space.
I won't stay on, if you want to keep him company until he dies, that
would be a humane and beautiful thing to do, but I can't; I'm
leaving tonight for Mexico City to request a visa so I can be with
your brother as soon as possible, maybe I can get one in time for
Christmas; I'm absolutely furious, I know I hurt him something
awful, but I am what I am, and I no longer have any respect for
him, in fact I despise him, deep inside I feel like telling Samantha
Valdés all about it and letting her cut him to pieces. Mama, please
don't do that, I'm begging you, she wailed disconsolately, then
paused the time it would take to read a sonnet; did you tell Aramís?
Francelia had learned about her mother's sexuality when she was
fourteen and it got her all mixed up, but in the end she came to
accept it. I'll tell him when I get there. And she knew her father
would follow the military tradition and take his own life. Can I
have a few minutes to think a little? she gave her mother a chilly
kiss and left the restaurant; she walked along the beach, and by the
time she returned to the hotel it was dark. She found María in the
lobby with her green suitcase, ready to depart, and she asked her
to wait. Then she ran into a group of drunk young women in wet

235

T-shirts. Some things in life repeat more often than necessary.

In the darkened bedroom she kissed her father on the forehead. I know you'll know what to do, Papa, she murmured, I hope you have what you need. Ugarte, without opening his eyes, pointed at the pistol on his abdomen and remained still. Could you tell me who you were? The best, honey, the best. *Yes*, in English, nodding firmly, she picked up her bag, and her voice vibrating with intensity: I love you, Papa, and if it's worrying you, believe me that I love you even more now. I do too, my precious, do you want to know what they called me? What? The bedroom was cold. Dog's Name. Like that? you weren't Odie or Beethoven? Just that. Why did you do it, Pa? Ugarte opened his eyes and fixed his gaze on the young woman with shining hair, his beautiful and haughty daughter. For love, it cut me to the core to see how your mother and I suffered because of that contemptuous swine, her scorn was beyond toxic. But why did you wait until now? Because I only got back two years ago, remember, for fifteen years I couldn't come any nearer than the border, and she was closely guarded; but suddenly everything fell into place, as if God had given me one final chance. Francelia resisted the urge to hug him and left without hearing him say: I did it for love, which is the only thing that explains your deepest needs. Taking his daughter's place, the shadow suddenly grew darker, more solid. Ugarte perceived the inescapable meaning and did not worry; from what he had seen so far, both of them knew how to wait.

Then, carefully, he got to his feet. María would have paid for the room for several days, but he wanted to return to the city of his birth. Why? If you cannot choose the place where you are born, at least you have that prerogative when you die. Ulysses and Moses returned home, didn't they? The shadow nodded softly.

He went out and took a taxi to Culiacán.

Forty-Five

December 23 was a special day. Mendieta, who had spent the previous night with Susana at his house and had agreed to try to make a go of it with her, arrived at the office thinking that everything was working out on its own, but he soon changed his mind. There was no Édgar Iriarte in the files of the Federal Police, the F.B.I. or Interpol. Zelda called the army but was told cuttingly: We don't give out information of any sort, especially about our own. By noon they were back at square one. Lefty, who had not thought about work matters all night long, felt a spark of regret, but the throbbing memory of red lips and a pinch from his body set him at ease, what could be worth more than that? Zelda, who had spent the afternoon with her boyfriend Rodo and her mother buying presents, and until midnight with Rodo alone, had also put everything out of her mind. Zelda's cell rang. Hello. It was Montaño. Agent Toledo, your voice is as lovely as the rest of you, a voice like that can only come from a good soul. The forensic doctor, who made love to every girl he met, had not lost hope of bedding Zelda, which is why she detested him. Cut the crap, doctor, what can I do for you? we're in the middle of a forty-four. I've got a present for you, I'll send it over. Oh, doctor, you shouldn't have bothered, who told you I like diamonds? As if you could ever seem like a bling-loving narco. They smiled. It's not much, seeing as it's for you, just a token of thanks for your friendship which I do not deserve. Fine, anything else? Is Lefty with you?

What's up, you fuck-maniac? Sorry for being out of touch, how are you feeling? Great, but what can you do, the pain is fading and the bruises too. No nausea or anything? Zilch, nada. The ribs, are they bothering you? Zero. Good, if anything comes up, like I said, you can call me anytime. Cavalry charge. O.K., see you later. Mendieta, answering his own cell. It was Pineda. Do you want to come over? we found four bodies and, by their white coats, they could be dentists.

Quiroz was waiting with a bag of Oma coffee and his usual incisive questions, tape recorder in hand. No doubt about it, Detective Mendieta, there is a serial dentist killer out there, what is your take on the case? Yes, everything seems to indicate the killer is a scaredy-cat journalist who's decided to liberate the mouths of humanity from that scourge. He turned off the recorder. You want me to put that out on the radio? Oh, I don't think so, you don't want to make me that famous. The times call for caution, Lefty, killings of journalists are more and more common and cruel. If curiosity killed the cat, imagine what it might do to a journalist. Reporters aren't stupid. But they take too many risks, you take too many. It's my job. So don't complain. O.K., then what's your theory about the murdered dentists, with these it makes six. Commander Briseño will tell you everything, call him, and thank you for the coffee. I remind you that you are my friend, and by the way I heard about your son, congratulations.

The bodies were north of the city in a thicket next to a cheap motel. They were spreadeagled on the ground and one was a woman. Pineda shared a few details and Ortega others: all of them murdered somewhere else with heavy-calibre bullets and then peppered here with a .45 after they were dumped. Montaño, who was working with two young assistants, told him that two had died the night before and the others that morning. The detectives took notes, Zelda Toledo scrutinised the scene and received the victims' personal effects from the medical staff, so she could contact their families and look for clues. Homicide as common crime, what a world.

Mendieta went over to Pineda. Anything about Tenia Solium that you haven't told us? From what I hear a toothache is killing him. That would be funny, not many nutcases could pull that off. Well, on your toes because arresting him won't be any picnic, he's a slippery bastard, and in this environment he's got the advantage. As far as I'm concerned he can fuck himself, he may be killing dentists, but I still think it's a case for Narcotics. No fucking way, he's yours, forget about us getting involved. You want to meet your grandchildren, right? More or less, tell me you don't, with that son of yours that turned up you must be thinking the same thing. No question about it, we live in the information age. Hey, did you say anything to Quiroz? Nothing, that's the chief's privilege. Good move; a few days ago a babe called me: her dentist got away from Tenia by the skin of his teeth, but nothing more happened. Alright, well, thanks for the heads-up. See you soon, Lefty what-a-sight. Pineda and his people pulled out.

Seventh Cavalry Charge. Any news, Lefty Mendieta? Be patient,

Samantha, there are a couple of gaping holes that won't close. I'm really anxious. Me too, sometimes the obstacles seem to be conspiring to overwhelm you, and you don't know which way to turn. Tell me about it; by the way, be a little more careful, last night when you left El Quijote you had a tail. What happened? Nothing, just be careful, at least until you solve the case, remember you promised me you'd have it sewn up by tomorrow. I did? She hung up.

The bodies were taken to the morgue, and soon the only people left were Zelda and Mendieta, all too aware they would have to face a hair-raising monster very soon. Lefty dialled Briseño and brought him up to date. What do you plan to do with Tenia? Send him chocolates for Christmas, what else? Let's hand the case over to the army or the Federal Police. Now you're talking, we'll go finish writing the report right now and execute your order. They climbed aboard the Toyota. Barely had they turned on to the highway when: Uh-oh. Mendieta saw in the rear-view mirror that a blindingly bright Hummer had been waiting for them at the exit from a motel. We've got a tail, Zelda, the kind you like. Zelda turned around. Not in my worst nightmare, adding after a moment, there are two, boss, a double-cabin is coming up behind; this dance is going to be good. She grabbed the two-way radio and requested backup just as the first gunshots blew out their tyres. The Toyota fishtailed to a stop, bullets bounced off the armoured glass and perforated the body, but not the armour. Boss, with these pistols we're nobody. On the floor there's an A.K., they gave it to me yesterday to hold for a minute and I kept it. Zelda grabbed it, opened the window and shot off half the magazine, shattering the windshield of one of the vehicles; the response came immediately: two A.K.s, emptied mercilessly. Zelda held back, alert, pumped with adrenaline: Damn them. Right then a blast from a Herstal broke through the Toyota's back window, not wounding them but defining just how far the balance was tipped. Oh, fuck. Mendieta recalled the horrible moment long ago when his car exploded and he flew through the air as it burned. Shit, the bullets continued to fly without pause. Boss, I've never told you, but I don't know how to pray, what do we do? Give me the A.K. and you take your pistol, we're going out; let these assholes know there are badges who aren't afraid of them. Are you serious? in other words, they're going to suck our dicks? What kind of language is that, Agent Toledo? don't lose your composure, especially if we're going to die. It's really too bad, boss, you were so excited about the mother of your son. Everything happens when it has to happen, Agent Toledo; when I say so, jump, we aren't going to die like rats.

The pursuers paused, then let loose another lethal volley. The detectives returned fire from inside, Zelda out the broken rear window and Lefty leaning out his door; it seemed as if their every attempt to confront the killers evoked a heavier response, until a tremendous bazooka blast from somewhere sent the Hummer flying and set it ablaze. Then a volley from a Barret ushered in utter silence. The detectives got out of the pockmarked Toyota holding their weapons in full view. They had run out of bullets. From the double-cabin pickup emerged a jubilant Devil Urquídez and Chopper Tarriba, the fucking bastards eating French fries and chugging beer. Everything O.K., my man Lefty? He had never smiled so widely. You'll have to forgive me, Chopper explained, my bazooka jammed, that's why it took me so long to shoot. I emptied the A.K. several times, but it didn't do the trick, added Devil. You two are pretty ugly to be guardian angels, but you turned up at the right moment. Orders from La Jefa, my friend Lefty, you know how she is. And who are these guys? pointing at the charred Hummer. Don't worry, I don't think it'll be long before we find out. Here come two black pick-ups, Zelda warned. They turned toward the vehicles racing the wrong way down the highway, several armed men aboard each. No shit, to one side an empty field and a small bullring. Are they ours? Nope, I don't think so, my man Lefty; let's go, Chopper. The boys went to their truck, Chopper picked up the bazooka and took cover behind the open door. Devil came back with pistols for the detectives and an A.K. for himself. They crouched behind the Toyota.

The pickups stopped about thirty metres away. A man got out, placed a rifle and a pistol on the hood and walked toward them, his hands in the air. It was Uncle Beto.

Which one is Lefty Mendieta?

Who wants to know?

Señor Valente Aguilar wants to speak with him.

The detective looked at Devil, who said nothing. Zelda shook her head.

You can come closer.

Here I come.

At his truck, Chopper, unblinking, trained his weapon on the nearest vehicle, while Devil pointed his own at the hired gun who, without lowering his hands, walked up to the Toyota.

You must be Lefty, my boss wants to speak with you. So, tell him to come.

The tension was right out of Stephen King.

He's dying, three weeks ago one of his teeth started hurting, but it's cancer, and now he can barely move, everything hurts. Hmm, these delicate guys are the worst.

He just got out, announced Zelda Toledo, whose eyes took in everything.

They turned and yes, Tenia Solium was making his way along the asphalt toward them, two men holding him up by the arms. Several cars stopped before reaching them, made U-turns and drove off. Except for one, which snuck up to the bullring practically unseen.

If you are as much of a man as they say you are, Lefty, you'll go and meet my boss, I'm asking it as a favour.

Tenia was moving slowly, stumbling. Very thin.

Mendieta started out and Zelda went with him. Devil signalled Chopper, then followed. Uncle Beto lowered his hands and walked in the lead.

Tenia had his head tied up with a blue kerchief. He stopped and swayed while the others approached. Zelda was calculating the possibilities of arresting them all, Mendieta had no idea what might happen. What kind of farce was this?

Face to face. Tenia, eyes black, glared at him. Lefty suddenly felt off balance, something that happened to him every so often, and he couldn't figure out how he'd ended up there, in such a weird situation.

You prick, do you know who was in that Hummer? Words tumbling out, voice barely audible, breath fetid.

Lefty withstood the stench without a word. Devil, rifle in hand, stood firm.

My son, asshole, you just killed my son, Lefty Mendieta.

The detective felt himself begin to recover, he breathed in deeply.

That's why you wanted to see me? what a pain in the butt you are, Tenia Solium.

The gunslingers holding up their boss felt him tense and then fold over.

Fuck your mother; my son, you bastard, a boy who was my eyes, what potential, what promise, you killed him on me.

You're a zero, Tenia Solium, and you're dying like a fucking mangy dog.

Enough, no more of that bullshit; just remember this, you fuckin' shit of a cop: for what you did to my son, I curse you, asshole, you're gonna die the worst death you ever imagined.

You already sucked my dick once, Tenia Solium, are you going to suck it again? how exciting.

Fuckin' Cat, you're worth shit, too bad you don't have any kids; 'cause I'd pay you back in spades.

Lefty froze, a strange sensation spread through him.

Tenia tried to spit at him, then indicated he wanted to be taken back. Devil, we'll settle accounts later, you shot at Valentillo, don't think I don't know it, and slowly he made his way to where his people were waiting. Cold gust. The detectives and Urquídez backed away without turning. Before Tenia managed to reach his vehicle and climb aboard through the pockmarked door, three pickup trucks appeared from behind, shooting at anything that moved. The Chúntaros had arrived. To the Toyota! Devil ordered.

Right then they heard a blast and a whining buzz over their heads; Tenia's pickup received a direct hit on the bullet-holes in the door, blowing the truck and all its occupants to smithereens. The hired guns who had been helping their murderous boss let go of him to return fire. Aguilar, a.k.a. Tenia Solium, was swaying like a cornstalk in the breeze, shooting wildly; and that was when the boss of the Chúntaros, a man in a black hat, took aim and emptied the magazine of his A.K. Tenia dropped his pistol and bit by bit, wounded all over, slumped to the ground.

Two minutes later, there were no more gunshots from Tenia's people. Several men from the last wave of pickups walked up, signalling toward the Toyota that the show was over, and gave each of their enemies a *coup de grâce*. The one directing the operation pulled a cardboard sign from his Cheyenne and laid it on Tenia's chest: *Rabbble, Dont be killin.*

In the Toyota the two-way radio was screeching. Zelda grabbed hold of it and reported that everything was under control, all they needed was the forensic doctor and several ambulances. The Chúntaros gave a wave goodbye, which Devil and Chopper returned, and sped off. What happened? Devil asked his sidekick.

The shot went off all by itself, it won't happen again, I don't think the bazooka's working right, first it jams on me and then the trigger gets touchy. Urquídez shook his head disapprovingly: You bastard, imagine if you'd missed Tenia's truck?

Mendieta was speechless when Jason, smiling ear to ear, got out of the car that had not driven off. What was the kid thinking? He felt his blood boil over, what was that snotnose doing here at a time like this? He suppressed an urge to give him a few good whacks with his belt, feeling at the same time shocked at his own reaction. Sorry, we were here by accident; the young man understood just how upset his father was. How could you do that? what, are you looking to get killed? They wrapped their arms around each other and squeezed, Zelda felt herself losing it, Devil could not believe any of it. Don't you ever go near a gunfight again, this mother's not like in the movies. Jason nodded gravely. One day I told my coach you were the best policeman in Mexico, Papa, he muttered, I don't regret it. Lefty did not know what to say. He thought, well, it's Christmas, such things could easily happen. He saw Gustavo coming over, accompanied by the girls, and he had an idea.

Forty-Six

Colonel Domingo Félix H. received them at his home office filled with shining trophies and diplomas: he coached the base basketball team made up of soldiers' children and the team rarely lost. Gustavo was the key that got them in the door, plus the colonel's curiosity about the personality they named and a few other things life teaches you. The chairs were uncomfortable, metal, cold; the desk was small and the coffee freshly ground and fragrant. Congratulations on your son, detective, he looks to be a very good kid. I would say the same about yours, I hear he's already chosen a career. I trust he'll become a general someday, something I never even got close to.

Night. Cold, but bearable.

Regarding the individual you are looking for, the first thing is that his name is probably not Édgar Iriarte, no military man with the profile you describe is called or was called that. He paused. It might be Héctor Ugarte, an exceptional case, an incredibly talented man; I can't understand why he didn't become a star, he had everything it takes. Did you know him? When I first started here he came several times to meet our commander at the time; he was friendly, very good-looking, a skilful conversationalist. He put a metal folder into Lefty's hands. Take a look.

Héctor Ugarte Rojo, rank: first captain, forty-two years old, intelligence and special services, married to María Leyva, a ten-month-old daughter, address in Las Quintas. Photograph.

Lefty did the calculations and figured he had just turned sixty, why did Samantha and Max think he was over seventy? were they wrong? was he the guy they were looking for? did he wear make-up? Wong didn't remember the name right either, could he be sick? a human being is an ambiguous beast. He read the two lines of *curriculum vitae*, which did not help in the least. Colonel, is he still alive? No idea, as you can see the information is bare-bones and it's all we've got on him. You have nothing from the past seventeen years? Don't get offended, but this is the only thing I can share without feeling like a traitor. Not even a new address? Nothing. Did he do rock-climbing or mountaineering? No idea. About five foot six tall. More or less, thin but strong, a bit effeminate. Any special name, any nickname? That I wouldn't know. Though it isn't much, I thank you for the information; just answer me one thing, why did you think of him? how did you know Ugarte might be the man we want? The colonel grimaced and got to his feet. The detectives followed suit, although not immediately. In the space of two minutes he seduced the girl I was going to marry: a bastard like that you don't forget.

What's the name of that character in Shakespeare who's an expert at making people jealous? Oh, boss, what would I know about that?

As soon as they got into Zelda's car, Lefty wrote down the facts he could not memorise. What do you think, boss? We're in the dark all over again, worth shit. That's what the President said: the Mexican police are incompetent, corrupt and unprepared. When did he say that? Last night, and I read about it today; listen, that was heavy with Tenia, wasn't it? his son getting burned to a crisp right there, and Chopper with the itchy trigger finger. A couple of bastards. They drove unhurriedly toward the address in Las Quintas, it was right near the Pacific Cartel's safe-house. Tomorrow is Christmas Eve. And then Christmas; are you going to have dinner with the family? Most likely. Boss, congratulations, and like you said the other day we've got to forget all about this zoo and have a good time with the people we love; we're going to have turkey with stuffing and buñuelos for dessert; we invited Rodo's parents, and I'm going to get my hair washed the way it should be, in a salon. Poor Rodo, you're going to make his head spin; I don't know what we'll eat but it'll be something special for sure, Susana owns a restaurant in Los Angeles. So she knows how to stir a pot. That's what Jason says. Silence. Do you have any hope this guy will be there? Nope, I'm not even sure it's him; the only thing we'll get out of this business will be more money for presents. There is that, thanks to your friends. Mendieta pretended not to hear, and he dialled Susana. How are you? Taking a nap. Nice, that's what good girls should be doing, did the gringo turn up? Not that I know of; you'll come for dinner tomorrow, right? Of course, we'll eat and we'll drink until our bellies turn blue. Are you at work? Affirmative. You should put in a request for vacation and we could go somewhere. Stupendous idea. I love you. So do I, goodnight. Short silence. It's great to be stuck on someone, right, boss? More or less. They breathed easy. A lot of traffic on the main streets.

The address turned out to be a one-storey house in darkness, garden abandoned, walls unpainted and discoloured. Don't even stop, Lefty told his partner, it's emptier than a country cemetery, and she drove slowly on. We can drop by in the morning not to leave it hanging. Mendieta studied the facade and as it left his angle of vision he saw a window grow brighter. Wait a sec, it looks like somebody's home, park wherever you can. They took their guns and walked back. The neighbours, maybe watching television, maybe sleeping, for sure getting things ready for the following day; through their windows, the blinking lights of Christmas trees. Devil and Chopper parked far enough away that they would not be seen.

Sure enough, a feeble glow was coming from the living-room window. They crossed over the nearly metre-high wrought-iron fence and squatted in the weeds for two minutes; a car went by. From the looks of it nobody lives here, hardly a family with a young daughter, Zelda muttered; the glow disappeared. Aha, somebody's there, the detective whispered, maybe not the man we're looking for, but someone just closed a door or turned out a light. What do we do? The simplest thing: we knock. Well, get to it, boss, I've got to pee.

Knock knock knock. After a long minute, guns at the ready, they heard feet dragging. Ugarte threw the door open. He looked very thin, very old and very sick, even in the darkness. They gaped at each other. Were you expecting someone? Not anymore, as you can see I'm in no condition to . . . he interrupted himself to examine them carefully; police? We're no big deal, but you are Captain Héctor Ugarte Rojo from military intelligence. He contemplated them. If you're looking at me, you must understand I can't ask you in, I'm really sick. That much we can see, put your hands in view, you're wanted for the murder of Mariana Kelly. The man breathed deeply, smiled as if a weight had been lifted from him. Lefty frisked him and led him back inside, behind them Zelda confirmed there was no-one else in the place. Ugarte asked permission to sit in his La-Z-Boy; Mendieta checked it over carefully. Zelda came back with a Smith & Wesson Classic, a five-bullet .38-calibre special with a three-inch barrel and a silencer. A jewel. I only have one question, Captain Ugarte: after you rappelled down, how did you manage to open the window to Mariana's room? The man felt better: this policeman was showing him respect, he wanted something only he knew. Through Samantha's window; she was in the shower; that's also how I left. Of course, that was what Lefty had perceived but could not work out: two windows right next to each other, leading to connecting rooms, he turned to Zelda who nodded. Did you know it would be open? No, I went there after I found Mariana's closed and thought I'd failed, then it was just a question of waiting. You must have had your reasons to do this job, Captain Ugarte. Nothing much, after so many years the only thing that remained intact was my hatred. Like Edmond Dantès? With the difference that I could never forgive. We found your climbing equipment, were you hanging there a long time? About eight minutes, Samantha wouldn't stop talking on the telephone and a young guard kept looking in my direction, maybe he was just watching a few gringas who were practically naked, I don't know, but all the same he could have seen my silhouette against the window; a couple of gunslingers making their rounds went by once boasting about their romantic conquests without showing the least interest in the wall, the overalls I used were the same shade of red. I can see you are a very patient man. Patience is an addiction; with all due respect, señor . . . They call me the Cat, Ugarte looked at him for a moment. You couldn't be the policeman who somehow survived an explosion about twenty years ago? Mendieta made a gesture that said there was no way around it. Dog's Name, that's what a lot of people called me; I was telling you, with all due respect, I would appreciate it if you would allow me to end this matter myself, that's why I have the pistol. Lefty studied him: Right, a military tradition. And look, I only did undercover operations, some of them were truly spectacular, but this one was personal and I would like people to know, so if you have any reporter friends and could do me the favour . . . Lefty smiled, made a gesture of understanding, went out into the garden and dialled Samantha Valdés.

I've got your man. Who is he, Lefty Mendieta? Héctor Ugarte, husband of María Leyva. Instant reaction: My God, I can hardly believe it. Should I give you the address or bring him to you? No, I'll be right there, Devil called Max a few minutes ago. Lefty paid no attention to a beautiful young woman with shining hair and a backpack, who paused at the gate to stare at him haughtily before walking on. Seven minutes later, the head of the Pacific Cartel stepped resolutely from a black S.U.V. Max, Devil and Chopper went inside with her.

She stood in front of Ugarte, who looked at her with that same peculiar smile of triumph. Zelda went outside to keep her boss company. So it was you, woman with balls, it never crossed my mind that I knew you, you looked so decrepit and with that moustache you stuck on. Because of you damned bitches my marriage was hell for years on end. You've got your ass on backwards, woman with balls. I spent fifteen years separated from my family because of your father. And I can imagine your witch of a wife must have missed you terribly, that shameless flirt. He looked at her contemptuously, in command, immaculate; the others watched. I beat you, Samantha Valdés, admit it; I took away what you loved most, just as you people did to me; now you know what it feels like to be utterly deprived of the one you love. La Jefa, whose face had fallen, signalled Max, who passed her his .45 with the safety off. Dry lips, trembling mouth. She took aim.

The afternoon of the 24th, following Trudis's advice, Mendieta went to Doña Mary's house to ask if he could bring anything for the meal that night and to take her a bouquet of pink alstroemerias. He felt happy, for himself, for Jason and for everybody else. The Jetta was parked outside. A dishevelled young man texting on his cell answered the door. What happened? She's like that, unpredictable, she uses me as an excuse but it's like with the Marine; she's the one who doesn't dare make a commitment. He reached for the flowers and set them on the table. You mean Susana's gone? She took the first flight out this morning. Lefty collapsed into a chair, he had spent all morning writing his report and depositing his money in the bank. Jason put a hand on his shoulder. Take it easy, Papa, that's how women are, they don't pick sides, they come and go. Mendieta smiled mirthlessly, ruffled the asterisks of Jason's hair and handed him a debit card. Your other present: there's enough there for you to study whatever you like, whenever you like, wherever you like. They hugged. Then he convinced his son to go have a good time with Gustavo and the girls. You are an idiot, his body muttered, utterly crushed, but then reassured him he would be alright.

At home he took the Bob Dylan C.D. out of the stereo and put on José Alfredo: "Qué Suerte la Mía". And he drank for hours until he passed out. Fuck it.

ÉLMER MENDOZA was born in Culiacán, México in 1949. He teaches literature at Sinaola Autonomous University and is widely regarded as the founder of "narco-lit", which explores the impact of drug trafficking in Latin America. He won the José Fuentes Mares National Literary Prize for *Janis Joplin's Lover,* and the Tusquets Prize for *Silver Bullets.*

MARK FRIED is a literary translator specialising in Latin American literature. He lives in Ottawa, Canada.